Nowhere Near

Nowhere Near

Stories
by
Teddy Jones

New York, New York

Published by MidTown Publishing Inc.
1001 Avenue of Americas
12th Floor
New York, NY 10018

Library of Congress Control Number: 2017906603

ISBN 978-1-62677-016-4 (print book)
ISBN 978-1-62677-017-1 (eBook)

All rights reserved
Printed in the United States of America
First Edition
1 3 5 7 9 10 8 6 4 2

Contents

Much Madness is divinest Sense -
To a discerning Eye -
Much Sense - the starkest Madness -
'Tis the Majority
In this, as all, prevail -
Assent - and you are sane -
Demur - you're straightway dangerous -
And handled with a Chain -

—Emily Dickinson, *Much Madness is divinest Sense*

"To the extent that this world surrenders its richness and diversity, it surrenders its poetry. To the extent that it relinquishes its capacity to surprise, it relinquishes its magic. To the extent that it loses its ability to tolerate ridiculous and even dangerous exceptions, it loses grace. As its options (no matter how absurd or unlikely) diminish, so do its chances for the future."

—Tom Robbins, *Even Cowgirls Get the Blues*

Acknowledgments

As always, my first reader, Dr. Martha Burns, deserves thanks for much that is good and worthy in these stories. She has read each of them in their many iterations, always with unfailing good humor and consistent criticism, both of which are beneficial to the writer and the stories. Nearer its final form as a collection, this group of stories further gained shape and polish from the UNM Summer Writers' Workshop in Santa Fe 2016 master class instructed by John Dufresne. Thanks to John, Kim Bradley, David Norman, Karen Kravit, Jason Harris, and Scott Jones. Your efforts made this better work.

Also due thanks are those publications in which some of these stories appeared previously in somewhat different form. Those include 94 Creations ("Across the Vermilion Border"), Realsouth Magazine ("First Things First"), and the Pirate's Alley Faulkner Society's Double Dealer ("Clean Getaway," which received the Society's 2015 First Place Gold Medal for Short Story).

And finally, thanks to Eleanor Morse, one of my mentors at Spalding University's MFA in Creative Writing program, who convinced me of the value of revision as a process of reimagining.

– Teddy Jones

Nowhere Near

Clean Getaway

Seems like longer, but it was only day before yesterday. A little after eight that morning, I parked my pickup close to the door and walked in the Farmer's Co-op office. It squats next to the truck scales, across the lot from the four hundred-foot-long row of grain elevators.

I spoke to Charlene, the woman who runs the scales and usually messes up using the equipment that draws a grain sample out of the load. Never looking my way, staring out the big window that looks out on the scales, she said, "Morning, Owen."

Just as well. I didn't want to get her to talking or she'd foul up a simple task like making out a weigh ticket on the load someone had just pulled up on the scales. Besides, I was thinking. So I poured a cup of coffee, sat down, and picked up the Amarillo paper which was already open to the page with the grain markets.

I was the first one there that morning, just waiting to see who turned up to play dominoes. Some of us come every morning to play a few games and talk. The coffee's not bad and the manager likes to see us older guys, the ones who own shares, "participating in the organization" as he calls it. Nearly nine-thirty and nobody there but me, Charlene, and the manager, back in his office. And then Joe Ben walked in.

I said, "Good you made it. Thought I might have to switch to solitaire."

He looked at the coffee cups on pegs over the pot, took down the red one Rip laid claim to some time back, filled it, and ambled over to the table. "You the lone ranger today?"

"Looks like." I checked to see if all twenty-eight dominoes were still on the table.

Joe Ben sat across from me. "This seat reserved?" He raised the red cup like a salute in Charlene's direction. From what I can tell, he fancies himself a ladies' man.

"Rip usually sits there, so I can keep an eye on him. He's shifty. No one's figured out how he nearly always manages to draw something he can set for a spinner right off. Could be these dominoes are marked." I laughed like that might be a joke. After shoving the dominoes around a little to mix them up, my version of shuffling, I said, "He hasn't turned up, wasn't here yesterday. So I guess you can take his chair."

He stared at the seven pieces he drew. I stood mine up in a row and organized them to suit me. Looked like a foot instead of a hand.

"We didn't draw for down," he said.

"Guess I was preoccupied." I pointed at his neat row of ivories. "You're sitting in Rip's seat, so you can down first. He always does whether we like it or not."

I pushed the bone pile to one side and looked again at my hand which had two single-spots and no more than two of any suit. Only one five count in it. I'd be drawing from that mess of extras, it looked like. "I heard you and the wife went south for a long vacation. That right?" Fact checking. I don't go to church and I'm boycotting the local paper, so the only news I get from here in town is gossip, most of it right there at that table.

Joe Ben gave me a shit-eating grin and laid out the six-four, making it thud on the table. "Want me to keep score?" he asked. "Your turn." He said it like I never played the game before.

"Sure, you keep score. I'll keep an eye on your sharp pencil."

He marked on the pad, me watching to see he only made one X. He said, "Gone two months. Harvested that little irrigated half-circle of wheat and left. The Hill Country sure beat the hell out of staying around here. I checked the weather in the Panhandle every day…"

I interrupted him. "Don't have to tell me it's been windy and dry. All us stalwarts stayed to watch it blow." My four-ace slid across the table without a sound and butted up against the four end of his ten-count. I tend not to make loud plays even when I do score. "Rip was saying the other day this was the driest stretch he'd seen in this country since the fifties."

"He'd know. What's he, about ninety now?"

I waited to see if he intended to play or just gloat about that piddling score. He laid out the double ace. "Made us a spinner," he said, like he'd accomplished something.

Joe Ben kind of aggravates me. Always has, ever since he was a little kid. He's about ten years younger than me. "Rip's ninety-three this year. You missed his birthday. Had a cake here that day."

"Yeah, when was that?"

"Same as every year we been haunting this place, June first."

Saying that helped me put my finger on it—not just that he runs irrigation water non-stop on most of his fields, although as a dryland farmer, I mistrust those guys. Joe Ben never thinks about anybody but Joe Ben. Doesn't come around very often, or show any concern for anyone—not like the rest of us who've slowed down on farming. He's one of those who'll never think he's slowed down, even when he gets my age. He'll keep on buying land and big tractors till the day he dies. You know the kind.

He probably didn't have any idea the oldest member of the Co-op, one of the founding members, had his birthday up here every year. This place has been through three managers in the past twenty years and every one of them keeps that going on. Or maybe it's Charlene and before her that woman who used to work here, the one was married to that pen rider, are the ones who do it. Always homemade and always chocolate.

"Where is he today? As I recall, he usually gets the first cup out of the first pot."

"Don't know. He doesn't check in with me." The ace-three would fit on that spinner, but no doubt Joe Ben had the double-six. So I played the six-trey and waited to see if he'd mark my five. He studied his dominoes, then pushed over the ace-six and slid it toward the spinner. I said, "Keeping score and playing may be too complicated for you. I made five."

"Oh, sorry. Hadn't played in a while." He drew a / under my name, across from his X. "You reckon something's wrong with Rip?" He was staring at his dominoes like he expected the spots to multiply. "How many years since his wife died?"

"The year I moved back out here." He never looked up when I answered. I doubted he was listening.

I said, "No domino games in Central Texas?" It didn't look like there was much of one there that day either. I was about to draw from the bone pile when I noticed I did have one play. "Could be a doctor's appointment. His daughter from over near Muleshoe sees he gets where he's supposed to be."

I didn't mention I'd stayed awake a long time last night after the helicopter flew over my house to land at the hospital. Lately, every time I hear that or find out someone had to be flown to the hospital in Amarillo, I wonder if it's Rip. Or someone younger. If I can't get back to sleep I end up wondering when it'll be my turn. I caught Joe Ben looking at me. "I know. It's my turn."

I connected the three-ace.

Joe Ben's phone played the opening sounds of "Born to be Wild." He grinned like he was the only one who'd ever had a motorcycle. He turned his back to me and answered the phone, almost in a whisper. "Why sure, if it's all right to come now, I'm on the way."

He slapped the phone in the holster clipped to his hip. That grin again. "Got to go. Seize the moment, as they say."

I could tell he wanted me to ask where, but I didn't. After he sailed out the door, I knocked over his hand. No double six. Damn. I'd been too cautious again. I finished my coffee, and put my cup back on its peg.

Making the rest of my morning rounds didn't take long—the post office box offered only an advertisement for hearing aids; I didn't see any extra vehicles at the funeral home;

and the girl at the drugstore found my blood pressure prescription refill without much chatter.

My final stop was the farm store. The owner's daughter frowned when she sold me six bolts, like anything less than a dozen was more trouble than it was worth. A bolt needed replacing on one of my old wheat drill's press wheels. Just for the hell of it, I said, "Put it on my bill." I ambled back to the coffee area, but the pot was empty and none of the usuals were hanging around. So I headed out to the farm, pretending that repairing the planter was an urgent matter. Fact was it wouldn't see use until September and with no promise of rain, and no irrigation, there was no sense in planting any milo.

I took my time driving the eight miles from town to the farm. Our family's old home place, the house, was all that was left except for my equipment. The barn and the chicken house and all the other outbuildings had been bulldozed into a pit and covered twenty years ago. I did that when I moved back here to operate the place. I had lots of ideas and plenty of energy that year. Only forty-eight and I felt free getting back home after working in Lubbock all those years for the Extension Service. Dad had died and it was either farm it myself or lease it or sell it outright. Something about selling it didn't seem right. Terry said, "Why not farm it? We'll make it an adventure." That's the kind of wife she was. When she died five years ago, seemed like my spirit of adventure went with her.

Even though we lived in town, I left the old house standing, mostly because I remembered when my grandparents lived in it. They had endured the Dirty Thirties and the fifties and all those other dry years. Plus a lot of good green ones, too.

Thinking about them, I sat in the pickup I don't know how long before I ever summoned up the gumption to get out and work on the wheat drill. I never saw the sense in going in debt for new equipment when I could make the old work. Almost every moving part on that planter had been replaced over the years since Rip sold it to me. More like gave it, for the price I paid. He'd said he didn't need it because he'd picked up a newer one at an auction, and besides, he wanted to help me get started. He sort of took me under his wing the first few years after we moved back. Never gave advice unless I asked, which I did. After several of the guys around here, some I grew up with, dropped comments about me being a "hobby farmer," I got pretty close-mouthed around everybody except Rip.

I should have been paying attention to the repair instead of entertaining recollections. The nuts off of six small screws fell out of my hand and scattered in the dry grass and goatheads below. "Damnation." And then I had to wipe the sweat off my bifocals to look for them and couldn't find my handkerchief. "If it's not one thing, it's two others."

So I buckled down, and close to noon, I finished, after stopping a couple of times to consider getting out my phone and calling Rip. I told myself he couldn't hear the phone and probably wouldn't answer if he could. And I thought I might drive seven miles farther north to his place. But I didn't.

On my way in, when I got near town, I slowed down while I tried to decide where to eat. The pickup must have a mind like an old horse. Before I knew it I was in the driveway at my house.

Yesterday morning I turned up at the Co-op before any other coffee drinkers, again. Then that fat Baptist preacher came in. I doubted he'd stay long—there weren't any doughnuts. I didn't offer to shuffle the dominoes. We passed the time about the weather while he drank a little coffee. Then he said something about me having a blessed day and left. I didn't tell him it felt that way already since he hadn't hounded me about attending services.

Before long, four more strolled in. I moved my chair back from the table and claimed to have no interest in the game they started. Using the newspaper as an excuse, I made out like a story on the front page had my attention. In fact, I checked my watch four times in thirty minutes. Rip never did come. One of the others asked me if I'd seen him. "Not since the first of the week," I said.

"I bet he's down at Muleshoe visiting his daughter. You know she's been after him to move to the nursing home there."

"Has she?" I didn't tell him what Rip had said that last day he was there.

Talking quietly that day, even though we were the only two left at the table, he'd told me. "She wants to get me in assisted living. Says she worries all the time that something might happen to me. You know what I told her?"

I recall shaking my head and keeping my mouth shut. He was going to tell me anyway.

"I told her it was more likely something would happen to me there than out here. Lock me in there and I'd shrivel up and die. She said they'd see I got regular meals. Thinks I don't eat."

"Do you?"

"When I get hungry." He had rearranged the dominoes in front of him. He said, "To satisfy her, I said I'd drink that stuff she brought."

"What stuff?"

"Ensure. Supposed to supply all the vitamins a man can use."

"That make her happy?"

"She wants me to wear one of those emergency buttons around my neck, too."

"Might be a good idea."

"I was born out there on that place and that's where I intend to die."

"You feeling bad?"

He looked around the room like it might be bugged. "Not particularly. She keeps dragging me to specialists. I go to make her happy."

"She's trying to help, I reckon."

"Yeah, reminds me of her mother that way." He looked off toward the row of elevators. He sat back, pulled the dominoes toward him, and picked one up, but didn't play it. He said, "I'll let you down first for a change."

We played two hands. He beat me like he always did. Managed to set a spinner on his first play both games and never had to draw from the boneyard. He pushed the dominoes into a huddle, about to shuffle for a third hand, then stopped. He pushed his chair back and said, "Want to take a ride out to the house with me?"

"Sure, why not?"

In his pickup, I had to toss seven—I counted—empty Ensure cans into the back to clear the passenger seat. "That stuff taste pretty good?"

"Only one I tried was the chocolate." He sneered and shook his head. "Nasty! I figure it'll please her to see empty cans. I pour out one or two a day. Save the cans and leave them in the trash for her to find."

"Sort of a game?"

"For me. She doesn't know we're playing."

He pulled onto the highway heading west and after a couple of miles turned onto the first county road north. "Why don't you just pour them down the sink at the house?"

"That's where I stack up the dirty dishes. Looks like I've eaten a lot since she was there last."

Remembering it yesterday morning, I thought I probably should have called his daughter, but he trusted me or he wouldn't have told me. At the time I thought it was funny.

He had stopped the pickup in front of his barn. "We'll get out here. I've been doing some clearing out and came across something that might interest you."

He didn't object when I offered to help him push the two eight-foot doors open. The barn is all metal with pole supports in the center and a concrete floor, probably sixty by sixty feet, maybe thirty feet high in the middle tapering down to twelve on the sides. Light filtered in through fiberglass panels on the roof and sides. The smell of grease and moldy grain made it seem familiar. Soon as I could see in, I wondered how the place looked before he cleared out.

He led me on a narrow path among the implement parts, a fifty-five gallon barrel—contents unknown, six two-gallon plastic bottles that had once held herbicides, a stack of wooden pallets topped by one sack of wheat seed—TAM 105 the label said, a jumble of shovels and hoes, past a Craftsman tool tower, a shop vacuum, and who knows what else he'd used or forgotten in ninety-three years. The story of an old farmer's life lay strewn like half-finished thoughts in that barn.

"Back here's what I want to show you."

There toward the far end, where there's a second set of doors, the floor was clear, free of the past's debris, freshly swept. A shop broom leaned at a weary angle against the right side wall.

"I never saw you drive that pickup before," I said. A dark blue 1991 or 92 Chevy crew cab pickup that looked near new owned the back end of that barn.

"Seldom did. Got it just before my wife died. Meant it to be hers. After she passed, I parked it. No one else knows it's here." He waved me closer. "That's not what I wanted you to see, though. Come around here." He led me toward the far side of the pickup. Getting past, single file, me behind, I heard him muttering. "That girl or her husband neither one ever been in here. Don't care about this place."

I kept my mouth shut. Until we got near the wall, I couldn't see what he was aiming for because the sunlight didn't reach there. He stopped after several steps. "That pickup makes me think. I was going to tell you something. But only if you swear not to tell anyone else."

Truth is, lots of things ran through my mind right then. Like I feel when I hear the weather alert on the television—wondering whether I ought to run or hunker down in place. "Something illegal or immoral?" The little chuckle I added turned out weak. Probably didn't fool him.

"Well, if you're worrying about bein' an accessory, you can stop."

The knot that formed between my shoulder blades let up a little but didn't relax entirely. There's no telling what people will do when they spend a lot of time alone with the past, trying to make plans for the future. Some take to religion. Others get concerned about enemies conspiring against them. And some, religion or not, tend to dwell on where they'll spend the afterlife. I've known others who wasted precious time thinking about who gets the land or money if there is any. All of those are sad, to me. But the saddest is when a person gets lost counting—rehashing the past, adding up insults, stacking up grudges, making lists of the few happy days in his life, finding nothing to equal the single high point that happened in tenth grade. I'd resolved a long time ago to try not to let myself miss out on today by thinking about "back then."

I had no real idea what Rip spent his time thinking about, except for what he'd told me that day. I pulled out my handkerchief and made a show of wiping my forehead. "That's a relief. Go ahead and tell me."

I'd gotten close enough that I could see, barely, the other things in that corner besides us. One looked like a big two bladed fan, but not exactly, and something else mechanical sat behind it, which I couldn't make out.

Rip turned around so he was looking squarely at me. "About my wife's pickup. Just in case my girl tries to ground me by taking mine, the keys to that one are under the floor mat." He pointed his crooked right index finger toward the blue vehicle. "Battery's good. I come out and turn it over the first of every month. I won't be surprised if she comes out and steals mine some night, just to make sure I don't get away before she can get me locked up. Badgered me until I gave her a set of keys." He took a deep breath and shook his head. "My own fault."

I thought then about asking where he'd go, and whether his daughter really would do that. Instead I just nodded my head and said, "Uh huh."

"I'm telling you in case you need to make a getaway someday, yourself."

"I'm much obliged." I backed up and looked in the pickup window. Neat as a pin. An air freshener shaped like an evergreen hung by a string on the cigarette lighter knob.

After a long silence, Rip said, "I concluded the other day I only have two real regrets."

"Not bad—only two in ninety-three years." I was trying hard to be good company and keep myself from wondering if hell might be cooler than that barn.

"Just two. First one is not having a son. That girl does her best by me, I reckon. But having a son would be different."

He didn't need to get stuck thinking about something there was no remedy for. So I said, "What's the second one?"

"Thinking of that made me think about you and I recalled that over there."

He waved toward the fan blade. "It's that I can't fly anymore. And I'm sorry I never told you before about when your daddy and I had a plane. Something a son would appreciate."

"You flew a plane?" Maybe I'd been wrong. Rip's imagination might be getting the best of him.

"Both of us, me and your dad. That's the propeller. Well, the one we had to replace after that crash. Come on over here."

We got close and sure enough it was a prop. And it had a missing end on one of the blades, which was twisted at a different angle than the other.

"That over there is the model we had a guy build later, after we thought better of being spray pilots."

I squatted to look at the miniature yellow biplane, complete with hoses and nozzles. The entire rig took up about four feet on the floor. I shook my head. "I never knew."

"You wouldn't. You were a little kid. Your dad about thirty. We got it in fifty-two, military surplus. We had some fun, made a little money in our short aviation careers." He reached down and spun the model's propeller. "Come here, I'll show you." He pointed to the front of the two single-file seats. "The pilot sat up here. We took turns. And the other one took hold of the blade and on the pilot's signal— *All clear* and then, *Give her a spin*—the one on the ground pulled down hard to get it turning and start the engine. "Then the ground man tore out to the pickup and drove fast to flag the spot to spray."

He caressed the propeller as if it were warm-blooded. His smile made me think that the memory of the two of them and their plane made him happier than he would ever be again.

"End of that year, one evening, we were both in the cockpit, just flying around the Panhandle, enjoying the scenery.

Next thing you know, the engine malfunctioned and we were headed down. We walked away, but the prop was done for.

"That same day both our wives said if we didn't get rid of that plane, they'd be gone." He stopped talking and fanned himself with his hand. "Damn, aren't you hot in here?"

"Thanks for showing me." We walked outside and pushed the doors closed. Then he drove us back to town, slowly.

I was focused on the day in that barn and other thoughts of Rip, when one of the four playing dominoes said, "You reckon we ought to go out and check on Rip?"

I heard him but didn't answer. The dream that woke me up last night also had me occupied. Rip wore goggles and sat in the front seat of that plane. He said, "All clear! Give her a spin, son." Then I woke up.

Another guy at the table said, "Maybe we ought to all go, in case there's something wrong."

I said, "He might get put out if we all went, looking like a delegation." I stood and folded the paper. "Since I'm not playing, I'll go." Walked out and didn't give anyone time to object.

Rip's pickup wasn't in sight in front of his house. No one answered when I knocked on the door or when I yelled. Walking out to the barn seemed to take me a long time. Instead of going in the front, I went directly to the back, calling his name, then pushed open the side of the door that stood partly open.

Finding him there didn't surprise me. But a heavy weight pushed against my chest when I stood over his body, lying there face down next to the open door of his wife's pickup. The keys lay on the floor by his right hand. "Rip!" The sound came out strangled.

I squatted to check for a pulse at his neck, which felt cool to the touch. Standing would have been a chore, so I sat down next to him. "I'm sorry you had to be here by yourself." It had all turned out just the way he wanted, so I guessed he hadn't minded as much as I did.

After I finished crying, I wiped my nose and got my telephone out of my pocket and called EMS. It would be okay to take their time, I told them.

This morning, the first thing I did when I left the house was go to the elevator. Charlene would have talked more after she said hello, but I moved on to the back fast enough to keep her from it. I poured myself some coffee in the red cup and sat at the table, pushed the dominoes around like someone was waiting to draw a hand. When the first one I flipped up was the double five, I knew what to do.

It didn't take long to find the box in the cabinet under the coffee pot. One by one I stacked the set of dominoes in the box and put on the lid. As I walked out the front door, I said to Charlene, "You're going to need to buy some new dominoes. These are missing one."

The funeral director eventually let me in the side door directly in the chilly room where they prepare the body, after I banged on it several times. He informed me viewing and visitation was scheduled for four in the evening. "I'm not here to visit. This is part of preparation."

Talking faster than I usually do, I said I'd been sent to put that box in the casket. He finally gave in after I showed him the box and said, "Family and friends' wishes. Dominoes." He hustled along beside me when I went over to the coffin.

His wide body blocked me from getting close enough. He'd started looking serious like undertakers will. He probably had the idea I'd let him take it from there, so he held out a hand and raised an eyebrow. But that wasn't my plan. Slick as a dancehall Romeo, I eased in between him and the foot of the casket. I said, "I'll slip it down here between his boots."

He backed away, muttered, "If you say so." I don't think he heard the keys when they clanked against the box.

First Things First

Carol Ann wasn't surprised Junior was the last passenger off the Continental Airlines flight from Houston to Lubbock. He would have sat, ignoring the scurrying in the aisles, until everyone else left from behind him. Then he would have stood and straightened invisible wrinkles from his suit and strolled up the aisle trailing his wheeled bag. She'd never been on a plane with him, but waiting, watching for him to pass through the revolving exit door, she'd imagined him going through that process. All his life, he'd cultivated routines as if they were prize begonias.

She caught him glancing around as he stepped from the passenger-only section, looking across the waiting area. He nodded when he saw her, like he approved. She was on time, didn't want to have to put up with his questions. From the time he was big enough to talk, he never settled for a simple answer about anything. With this headache, she was in no mood for his interrogation.

Maybe he didn't intend to sound like a detective; could be all research scientists talked that way. And whom did she have to compare him to? She didn't know anyone else who'd spent nine years going through medical school and the other education listed on his business card. Fellow, M. D., Ph.D, it said, Professor, Department of Physiology, Director of Gastrophysiology Research. He'd handed her one at the old man's funeral two years ago, like it was valuable. She'd left it in the bottom of her purse all this time until she dug it out and called him last week. The secretary who answered promised she'd pass along the message. Later, that same voice called back and told her when to expect him to arrive, today.

She stepped toward him, without thinking, her arms open wide, the way she greeted friends. He stopped just out of reach and turned around to adjust something on his luggage. "Did you have a good flight?" she asked.

"Routine. Some wind to be expected out here. Made it bumpy."

"Good it was on time." She hurried to walk beside, rather than behind him. He strode toward the exit, as if he knew where she'd parked. "You don't have any other bags?"

He shook his head. "Where?" That was her brother's way of admitting he couldn't locate the pickup.

She stepped around him, leading now, a two-person and one trailing-bag parade, toward the long term parking area. He said, "Long term?"

She nodded and wished she hadn't. Every movement jarred the pain from the back to the front of her head, like her brain might be sloshing, spongy in her skull. Count on one of these headaches to attack anytime she needed to be at her best. She couldn't safely take another extra-strength acetaminophen for an hour and a half, according to the small print.

She pointed toward the gray '91 Chevrolet pickup in the first row to her right.

"You're driving that?" he said.

"Sorry, Junior, my Mercedes is at the dealership for repair and I gave the chauffeur the day off."

"Please don't call me that. I prefer Charles."

"Maybe I'll call you Dr. Carson. Would that suit you better?"

She walked faster. At the pickup, unlocking the door, she took a close look at his bag. "That's going to have to ride in the back."

She wanted to laugh at the expression she'd caused. It made him look like a constipated old man. He said, "My notebook and phone are both in there."

"I guess you can hold it on your lap. That's what Mama does these days. Keeps her purse in her lap all the time."

She left him making fussy movements getting his gadgets, unzipping and zipping compartments, and got in the driver's side. As she opened the door, the odor overtook her again. The first time it happened, that exact smell had ambushed her while she was lying down with her eyes closed. It threatened to smother her. She'd been afraid to look, afraid the air would be bilious yellow, thick enough to see. The same sick fog assaulted her several more times, usually when she tried to get some sleep, times when Mama quit calling for her for a few minutes. Then as quickly as it came, the odor went away, didn't return until last month.

Junior situated himself, buckled up, and said, "What's in it?"

It took her a few seconds to figure out what he meant. "Her purse? Last I looked, her billfold with her driver's license, a bunch of Kleenex, and both of the letters you sent since the funeral."

"How long will it take to get there?"

"Haley's still sixty miles north of here. Hasn't moved." She stopped herself before adding the rest of what she thought. Being hateful to her brother wasn't going to get her anywhere. The air in the pickup had returned to dust-edged normal. She did give him credit for turning up. So she parked a smile in front of the headache.

Leaving the airport lot, she said, gesturing toward Lubbock, "See that crane over there? Big construction going on at the Med School, I hear. That other one's a new heart hospital."

She made a right turn onto I 27 North. A quick glance at Charles assured her nothing had changed. He looked the same as he had for as long as she could recall; erect posture, both ears covered—used to be tiny headphones connected to a Walkman, now it was ear buds—phone in his hand, vertical wrinkle between his eyes. Somewhere else, no matter where he was.

Looking straight ahead, as if it would make the trip faster, he asked, "What exactly is wrong with her?" The ear bud cord dangled below his chin like an afterthought.

"Doctor says she's fine." She watched the flat, straight highway. "He doesn't live with her."

When she pulled in the driveway, he said, "Here? I thought you were with her at the home place."

"My house is larger." A musty odor of mildewed unwashed underwear, the smell that had rushed at her from Mama's bathroom at the home place nauseated her. She swallowed to keep from vomiting. After a couple of breaths, she said, "I'd rattled around alone since Albert died."

"What about the home place?"

"I took you at your word. Handled it. Had to get rid of it all—land, house, equipment. Our old man left debts." She pushed on the pickup's cranky door handle and finally got it open, but didn't move. "No, that's not the full truth. He'd stashed twelve thousand in an account with his name on it, she didn't know about. But doctor bills ate that up when she started..." She stared out her side window. "Well, you'll see."

He made no move to get out. He inhaled through his nose, sort of a tuneless whistle. He said, "I got all I wanted a long time ago, my education. I remember telling you that." He continued sitting, focused on something too far away for her to see. "That and I got out of West Texas." He moved the phone from his lap to his jacket pocket, and rolled the ear buds and cord into a neat handful. "I would have helped with the sale. You should have told me."

"You could have asked." She pushed the door open wider, but didn't get out. "I didn't see a need to bother you. Not until now."

She slammed the pickup door and left her brother sitting in the passenger seat, eyeing the place like he was an immigrant newly arrived in West Texas. She walked in, heading toward the kitchen. The woman from Home Health, watching through the screen door, trailed her through the house until she stopped.

Charles and his bag eventually got as far as the living room before a beep from his phone took him back out to the porch.

She shook her head and tried to catch the drift among all the bits the aide recounted from her three-hour stay with Mama. "Moaned and would not be comforted. Did not need to pee when I got her into the bathroom. Kept asking where you were. Never took anything I offered to drink." Nothing new, so Carol Ann nodded, then nodded again.

She assured the aide she knew how hard it was. God knows it was the truth. "You kept her from falling. That's the main thing. I'll get her settled down." Charles came in the front door as she opened it to urge the aide out. He mumbled a word, maybe "Hello," as he passed.

"Thank you for your help," she said. "I'll send your check to the agency."

Her mother called her name, "Ca-rol Ay-unnnnn," a high-pitched wail of a sound with too many syllables. Louder each time, three times, before she reached the bedroom, the one that had been the master, which had the connected bathroom that made everything a little easier.

Carol Ann slowed at the doorway and said, "Mama, soon as I pee, I'll be right in to help you. I brought you a surprise." Said it loud enough for Charles to hear, if he was listening.

No matter how quickly and quietly she tried to close the bathroom door, the cat managed to get in, as if he had treasure buried in the litter box under the sink. "Bert, one of these days I'm going to lock you outside, clear outside. Coyotes will eat you."

Bert was her mother's cat, one in a long line of strays Mama took in over the years, and was in no danger of becoming varmint food. She didn't want her mother grieving over a missing cat, on top of everything else. She was thankful he was the only one she'd been able to corral when she moved Mama here. The other four probably had ended up coyote fare.

The cat levitated from the floor into the bathtub, landing with a soft thud. Carol Ann closed her eyes and gave thanks that the headache now occupied only a quarter of her skull. She needed her one remaining wit to get her brother to agree. She couldn't let him leave until they made a plan. She opened her eyes. Bert glared at her from his new perch on the far side of the tub, watching her wipe, then jerk up the elastic waist of her pants, and wash her hands. Just watching, as he had every day, all day, for the past three weeks. Carol Ann turned her back, then stood straight, and walked out. Let him have the room.

At first, she'd ignored the staring. But after a week or so of his constant scrutiny, it came to her. She remembered Chester, her husband's barn cat, following him around, staring like that, for weeks. And then suddenly he died—Albert, not the cat. Chester left right after the ambulance took the body away. Never came back. As soon as she put it together, she knew she was next, not Mama. And in that moment, she knew what she had to do.

Only on that day, and only once, did she allow herself to dwell on the unfairness of it. She made it all worse by making a list, thinking it would help her see what needed to be done. Items stacked up, a weight heavier than when she began. Here she was, only fifty-nine, young enough to finally have a few years of life, if she could get out of the house, but now struck with something terminal; Mama, near eighty, self-assigned to bed, needing constant care, losing her faculties. No children—Albert hadn't liked children and she'd agreed, thinking that gave them freedom; no savings and no excess money—thank the Lord for Albert's railroad pension, the only thing that kept her and Mama off food stamps.

She hated whiners. That was one of the reasons she no longer had any women friends. Who wants to listen to someone complain? And that's what most of them did if they visited, whined about their husbands, or about their ungrateful kids. So the day of the list, she told herself the only thing left to do was just get on with it. No one ever said life was fair. Damn it. And damn that cat.

Charles had to agree, no matter what it took for her to extract a promise that he would take care of Mama after she died. At this point, she figured it would be a few months, maybe even a year before she'd be useless. That would give him time to get used to the idea. For once he was going to have to join up, act like a part of the family. He might have to fake it, but he owed that much to Mama.

Her brother stood near the bed, saying something to Mama. Carol Ann couldn't catch every word, but their mother's face told her all she needed to know. Instead of the slack, vague expression she'd worn since she moved her in, their mother glowed, smiling and ruddy. With her right hand she fussed at her hair. She never let Carol Ann brush it, so it stood out from her head like a frizzy halo, the back pasted against her skull. "Look who's come home! My boy."

"I picked him up, Mama. At the airport."

"When's supper?" This, from the woman who ate only if hand-fed, and who stopped leaving the bed to come to the table sometime last year.

She could see Mama estimating whether she had time to get dressed before making it to the kitchen. Or maybe she forgot the location, given that she'd not gone anywhere in the house other than the bathroom, and then only when leaning her full weight on Carol Ann, in nearly a year.

"I'll let you two visit while I get supper together."

Mama said, "Carol Ann, would you turn that television off so we can hear ourselves think?"

In the kitchen she banged the cabinet doors, covering the sound of the two voices from Mama's bedroom. She couldn't remember Mama making an effort to chat with her, it had been so long. She'd only groan and call out, "Carol Ann," non-stop. Now, she'd remembered how to converse.

Carol Ann stopped still and gripped the kitchen counter. The headache snaked around the back of her head and grabbed at her neck. That's what you get, thinking hateful thoughts.

She set the table, organizing the points she would use to convince Charles. Mentally rehearsing the words she'd use. He wouldn't have needed convincing if he'd seen how quickly Mama had gone downhill from being the woman he remembered—the one who made sure he had everything the old man begrudged him—science camp in summer, special course schedule for gifted students, and an exemption from P.E. for his asthma.

Carol Ann knew about those things, but there had probably been many more. Being eight years older, she spent her time on other things when he was a little kid. After she dropped out of nursing school to marry, Junior crossed her mind only if Mama told her about some prize he'd won. Back then she knew Mama would stand between the old man and him and see he got a scholarship. Sure enough he did, Rice University, Houston, Texas.

Later on, Carol Ann wondered if her leaving helped, gave Mama one less person to tend. She guessed Junior never knew that until his birth, her Daddy actually laughed once in a while. It was like each one of them was an only child, from two different sets of parents. Daddy had suddenly turned old and sour. She would never know what caused the change. Mama wouldn't speak of the old man after he died.

She opened the refrigerator and a foul odor, rank and acrid, clouded the room. Her eyes stung as the smell of pig manure that always coated the old man's boots and clung to his clothes nauseated her. She shut the refrigerator slowly, hoping not to disperse the odor further. Supper might be a soup from a can tonight.

When she managed a rational thought, she knew rotten food wasn't the problem. Phantosmia. Easy enough to find when she looked on the Internet. Junior wouldn't believe it, so she didn't include among her points even a whisper about that or the headaches and the brain tumor she knew caused them both. If she saw a doctor, got a diagnosis, they'd want to treat it. She wouldn't be in any shape then to convince him to do his duty.

A few seconds later, the smell of the old man's work clothes receded. Everyone else out here raised cattle. Why had he persisted with pigs?

She pulled three potatoes from the pantry and a package of chicken breasts from the refrigerator. Junior only ate chicken, no other meat at all. That asthma attack when he was ten, which nearly killed him, started the day the old man made him help clean the pig pen. While he was in the hospital, the doctors tested, found out he was allergic to pigs—dander, hide, meat, the whole hog. Mama put her foot down after that. No more meat or outdoor work for Junior. Carol Ann left for nursing school soon after that.

Two voices continued from the bedroom, both cheerful. The headache released its talons from her neck.

Mama stood next to Junior in the kitchen doorway, leaning on his arm, more for show than support, it seemed. Carol Ann knew her face might give away her surprise at seeing the invalid so perky, so she bent over the lettuce lying in the dish drainer. "Tell me where you put my clean housedresses and I'll make myself decent for supper," Mama said. Junior might have had a question, but didn't say anything.

Without looking up, Carol Ann said, "They're on hangers in your closet. I'll come help you get dressed soon as I chop these tomatoes."

Bert purred his way into the room, passing between Mama and Charles. "Oh, there's my good kitty. Where have you been, Bert?" Mama said. "Junior can get my dress, and I'll get it on myself. Bert smells chicken, don't you, big boy?"

The cat stalked toward Carol Ann, stopped about a foot away, then curled into a tight black wad, facing her, flicking his tail. Staring.

She heard voices again from Mama's bedroom, followed by laughter. If she slipped out the front door, tiptoed off the porch, then tore out of the driveway, she could be in Amarillo before anyone would look for her.

After setting the salad, a bottle of Wishbone Italian, a bowl of green beans, the plate of fried chicken, and the bowl of mashed potatoes in the center of the table, Carol Ann looked around for her purse. Running away without a purse made no sense. Well, what did make sense these days? "Supper's on the table," she said. Then she repeated it, louder, so they'd both hear.

Mama put some of everything on her plate. Carol Ann waited to see if she expected someone to feed her, they way she had yesterday and all the days before. Charles started right in, cutting his chicken into pieces, not stopping until he reduced the whole breast to a mound in the center of his plate. Meanwhile, Mama forked up two green beans and bit of mashed potato and smiled toward Carol Ann. "I might need a little help cutting this chicken." Her voice sounded a little like Betty White, kind of perky. Carol Ann cut the chicken into small pieces and wondered if her brain tumor could be affecting her hearing, too.

After she took the acetaminophen at seven o'clock, she wanted to go to bed. The headache now covered her forehead and extended to the middle of each cheek. Surely Mama's sudden burst of energy had worn her out, too. But first she had to talk to Charles alone. If he thought Mama today equaled Mama all other days, she had to clear that up. He had to know the facts of the situation.

The three of them clustered in Mama's bedroom. She'd insisted her television had the best picture. And rather than return to bed, their mother sat in the rocking chair, the two of them sitting on dining room chairs, one on each side of her.

Carol Ann glanced sidelong past Mama and saw her brother had ear buds in place connected by a wire to something in his lap, although he faced the television. Mama followed the action on the old *I Love Lucy* with a satisfied expression, laughing in all the right spots. Watching the two of them, Carol Ann felt this must be how it is when a person greets an astronaut returning from space. Or in Junior's case, maybe meeting an alien. Mama had certainly been away. But today she returned! All the more reason Junior had to agree to a plan. With her dead or in the hospital, who'd see after Mama?

Her mother's head drooped forward a few times and then she snored. Carol Ann stood without making a noise and beckoned to her brother to follow her. Outside the room, speaking just above a whisper, she said, "We have to talk tomorrow. There's lots you need to know and we need to make decisions."

"I have a three-thirty flight."

"First thing in the morning, then. Maybe she'll sleep late. Try to ignore when she calls out in the night. I always get up when she does." She saw Mama's head move. "I'll see if she's ready to get in bed. I am."

Her mother protested she wasn't sleepy, but did agree to watch TV from bed. Carol Ann supervised as Mama used the walker to get to the bathroom where she said to leave her while she did her business. Carol Ann shook her head thinking of how many times in the past months, she'd had to put her on the bedside commode. It would feel good to just slap her, once.

Carol Ann woke, startled, gasping. Her heartbeat in her ears muffled all sounds. Had Mama called? She waited, heard nothing except her pulse. A smell she recognized filled the room. The only description she could muster was "old woman's crotch." That combination of urine and yeast and faint decay that lingered when an old woman left a bathroom. She lifted the bedspread and sheet. She could be the source. No, not yet, she told herself. The clock showed six, the longest uninterrupted sleep she'd had in months. "Give thanks for small favors," she muttered as she put her feet on the floor. Today she had important things to do.

As her pulse returned to normal, the headache slid into place behind her right eye and across the top of her head. She made coffee, took another Tylenol and waited. Waking her brother would be rude. And she hoped her mother would sleep until noon. Fat chance of that.

Charles came into the kitchen so quietly she jumped when she turned to find him staring in the cabinet. "Coffee cups?"

She reached in front of him and handed him one. "Coffee's fresh. The second pot."

He poured a cup and sat at the kitchen table. She blurted out, "We have to make a plan, now. About taking care of Mama when something happens to me."

"When?"

"Anytime now." She'd expected that as soon as she started, he'd ask questions like a detective and turn everything around on her, object to anything she suggested. Her head began throbbing. Maybe she had an aneurysm, not a tumor.

"No, you said when, not if."

"You were like this when you were a kid. Always picking at what people say, pulling apart every word." She put her elbows on the table to brace her hands, holding her head. She didn't look up as she said, "Listen to all I have to say and then, if you need to, ask your questions."

He didn't protest, so she spilled out what she'd rehearsed. "I'm going to die and Mama's going to outlive me." A quick look at him told her he was at least listening. "She needs to be looked after, not be left alone. That's the worst thing, being left alone. Even now I can't do all she needs. I can't afford more help. It costs a hundred and fifty a day." The expression on his face hadn't changed, as if he hadn't heard a word. "Promise me you'll see she's taken care of."

When she paused for a breath to keep from breaking down, he didn't say a word for a long time. Then he pushed his chair back from the table, stood, poured himself more coffee. Then he sat at the table again.

Speaking slowly, almost gently, he said, "Mother doesn't have to be a complete invalid. I agree with her doctor. There's nothing major wrong with her physically. And her mental status is within normal limits for her age. You're letting her take advantage of you. Make her do things for herself. Come to the table to eat."

Carol Ann didn't let herself laugh at that. She closed her eyes against the light that suddenly seemed twice as bright as usual. "She'd starve herself. End up with bedsores rather than get to the bathroom. If you'd been here, you'd believe me."

She opened her eyes and watched her brother sip his coffee. He said, "I'm here now."

"It doesn't matter if she's taking advantage of me. Not now. You still have to see she's taken care of when I die. I don't have money and she has nothing. Say it; say you'll take care of Mama." She had to stop speaking or she'd cry.

"Do you want to die?"

She shook her head, then hesitated. "Maybe." There, she'd said it. "But just take my word for it. This isn't about me. It's about Mama."

He nodded. "About Mama. But I need to know why. Tell me."

She could see he wasn't going to promise unless she did. "I have constant, terrible headaches and smell awful odors I know aren't there. That's a seizure and a brain tumor causes it. I looked it up. Or it could be an aneurysm."

His mouth made a thin, tight line as he leaned toward her. "Web MD, right? Whoever invented that shouldn't be allowed to practice medicine. Lots of things, non-fatal things, can cause those symptoms. Have you been to see anyone about this? What's your blood pressure? How much sleep do you get?"

She signaled stop, both hand pushing toward him. "None of that matters right now. I'll see a doctor after I know Mama's going to be taken care of."

"You know I will."

"I know no such thing. Not until you say you promise."

"There must be something else. You're too smart to believe the worst on the basis of something on the Internet. That's ridiculous. What is it?"

She shook her head, trying to think a way to say it that didn't make her sound like a fool. "The cat stares at me. They stare at people who are near dying."

Junior stared at her.

"See, I knew I shouldn't tell you. I wanted you to agree about Mama without me telling you any of that. You should take care of Mama after I'm gone, do it because you want to for her. I don't need pity."

He shook his head, then cleared his throat and leaned toward her. "I promise I'll take care of Mama."

It didn't matter to her that he sounded like he might be talking to a crazy person—choosing his words, speaking slowly.

She took a drink of her coffee and felt the headache move to a new location, a small space over her left ear. "She'll go back to the way she was as soon as you leave. Please tell her you'll be back. And say when. A person needs something to look forward to just to keep from giving up."

He looked at his telephone, swiped at the screen a few times. "According to my calendar, I have two days open next month. I will come back then."

Carol Ann thought something else important needed saying, but she couldn't come up with anything. It could wait until next month. "I'll fix some breakfast. How do you want your eggs?"

"Son, could you bring me some coffee?" Mama called.

Without a word, Charles went to the coffee pot, poured a cup, then headed toward the bedroom. Bert jumped up as if he'd been poked, and trotted off toward the sound of Mama's voice.

The Secret Agent's Daughter

"My father was a spy. Until last year, I thought his only steady work was as a son-of-a-bitch. Even that didn't seem to qualify as a full-time occupation." I spilled out those words in a whisper to the woman who chose the seat next to me. She had asked where he'd been working when he died. I had hardly looked at her before I spoke. Something about the way she'd immediately taken my hand and patted it, and the scent of her Tabu, must have reminded me of Mother.

The woman nodded, although she raised an eyebrow. By that time, I had deduced that's how people treat the daughter of the deceased at an occasion like this, as if I were not responsible for anything I said.

Visitation, the funeral sales representative called the event when my brothers and I made the arrangements two days ago. We were sitting in his office at the Beasley and Owens Funeral Home, the largest in Fort Worth. He explained that friends and family would wish to pay their respects and offer condolences to the family. My older brother, Kent, who'd chosen O and B, said, "Will food be served, and liquor? He would have wanted his friends to have a drink in his honor." Kent sounded as if needed a drink.

The salesperson's nostrils had flared before he rearranged his features. "Family wishes are always observed to the extent possible. However, we permit only wine on the premises. No catering is provided by our organization, although we can coordinate with a caterer of your choice." With a move as swift as a magician's he produced, from somewhere—maybe up his sleeve—a list of caterers, printed on beige cardstock. I watched him check his cufflinks while my brothers looked at the list.

So here I was, with this woman I'd never seen patting me, now on the arm, and peering at me, her right eyebrow raised. I took it as a gesture of sympathy. And I wondered what had caused the words to rush from my mouth. I had never told anyone. Could be I frowned when I drew my arm away. I asked, "Do I know you?"

She said a name that sounded like Mart. "I was a friend of your mother's from way back. I never saw her obituary, or I would have been at her funeral, too. We spent a lot of hot, dry West Texas days together. She'd want me to be here."

I reached for a tissue—a box of them, pastel, stood on the end table next to me, part of the visitation package. My mother and father had divorced more than twenty years ago when I was seventeen and my brothers nineteen and fifteen. And Mother died five years ago. How the hell could this woman know anything about her wishes?

Mart, whatever her name, leaned back in her chair. I watched her shift her focus to the rest of the room. I had a feeling she might be choosing her words carefully, like someone undercover. Without looking at me she said, "Your mother would have wanted to make certain he was actually dead and buried." She returned her full attention to me. "Our friend Alma once told her that bastards like Reese Murray never die." She made a "hmph" sound, and a wrinkle between her eyes showed for a second. Then she patted my hand again. For some reason, I doubted what she said, but I couldn't put my finger on exactly why.

I sat forward in my chair, looked at my watch. Only seven-thirty. The room belonged to us and the caterers until ten. The price difference for three hours as compared to two was so slight that Kent booked for three. "My people will be there, and they'll want to stay and talk. Some of them knew him," he said.

I wondered how.

I didn't know what to say to the woman, and she didn't seem inclined to leave. The only way to make myself sit quietly

was to let my mind drift. Just as well. It looked like this was
Kent's show.

It wouldn't do to lean back and close my eyes until it was
over. So I searched the room for my younger brother, Tommy.
No telling where he was. Over drinks last night at my apartment,
he interpreted Kent's liquor question to mean that a) Kent
would order his minions to attend and b) he wanted alcohol
served because his wife didn't allow it in their home. With a
double vodka in hand, he said, "If pushed, Kent can blame it on
the old man." Then he changed his voice to sound exactly like
Kent's salesman-sincere baritone and said, "It was his dying
wish." He stopped talking long enough to polish off his drink.
"His dutiful wife will believe him, either way." He jiggled the ice
in his glass. I ignored his signal. "Suits me," he said. "As long as
he's paying. I like a good California red."

His assessment was probably spot on. When he went
silent, I walked to my little kitchen and came back with a tall stiff
drink. I handed it to him, and wiped the ring from his glass off
the end table. If I don't look at him when he talks, I could
believe it was our father speaking. Same flood of syllables, same
sardonic wit.

Tommy's nothing like Kent. He spends his money as fast
as he makes it. He thrives on roving between jobs. As soon as he
competes for a new position, and gets a promotion or two, he
looks for the next one. He's been in so many jobs in all the years
since college, and in so many different fields, that I lose track.
I've learned not to be surprised when he shows up between jobs
needing a place to stay. At least he doesn't have a wife and kids.
He's not hurting anyone.

I had watched him study his empty glass, probably
pacing his intake for my benefit. I said "Kent mentioned some
of his people knew Reese. How?"

"Kent lies, says whatever suits the occasion. Don't
believe it." Tommy said it with a certainty that told me there
would be nothing further on that topic.

But still. Maybe back before he retired, our father sent
some people to help Kent get his business started, or people

who needed work between covert assignments. A thousand possible reasons. I mentally catalogued the information, labeled Kent's comment as possibly reliable and filed Tommy's as speculation. It's a habit of mine; we librarians can't help ourselves. Information must be amassed and organized.

I reprimanded myself mentally. I'd let my mind wander too long. This evening was part of the ritual. People were here. I should act my part, the efficient daughter who takes care of everything. Focusing my gaze above the closed casket that sat, like an expensive decorator accessory, behind a pair of overstuffed chairs near the back of the room, I stared at the spotlighted arrangement of Dutch iris and birds of paradise on a pedestal behind it. The flowers caused the only actual disagreement among the three of us when I chose them. Kent had said, "No, roses would be more appropriate," as if he were speaking to his simp of a wife. I knew their fragrance would smother me.

Tommy spoke up, as always, grabbing any plausible opportunity to trump Kent. "Fuck appropriate. She can choose what she wants. I mean, she's willing to pay for them. Aren't you, Sis?"

I nearly laughed at the expression on the funeral director's face. More than his nostrils flared. His eyebrows shot up, eyes widened. One thing, maybe the one thing, I can count on Tommy for is backup, at least when he's in the vicinity.

I was relieved to see the flowers seemed like they would last until the service the next day. And the casket, I wondered if he was really in there. More often than not, he had missed family gatherings, and when he did attend, he caused some kind of uproar. The lack of turmoil in the stuffy visitation room made me wonder.

Kent's voice intruded from somewhere behind me. I heard him say, "Yes, he was a unique individual, always ahead of his time, and probably misplaced in the small town he grew up in. I grew up there, too. You know, he's the one who taught me to fly. And he was a premier salesman. Could sell anything from kitchen appliances to complicated electronics. He was responsible for my going into sales."

A man whose voice I didn't recognize said, "He must have been proud of you. Selling more personal aircraft last year than anyone in our company's history put you at the top of the heap for sure. Any dad would be proud."

No answer from Kent or from his wife. Without looking, I knew she'd be standing next to him, as always. As far as I knew, Kent hadn't spoken to our father in fifteen years. His wife made clear Reese Murray was not welcome in their home after he turned up with a child-sized electric Jeep for their son's first birthday—the child could barely walk and certainly couldn't drive the miniature vehicle—and got drunk at the party in front of her family and all their assembled friends. At the time, I didn't really blame her. But, fifteen years! You'd think a born-again Christian would forgive.

Reese Murray loved buying toys, the more complex the better. But he always expected children, us especially, to be smarter and more capable than we were. I remembered the telescope he'd bought my brothers when they were still kids. They spent even less time looking through it than they did experimenting with the chemistry set from the year before—almost none. Dad must have wanted one as a child; he spent hours with it.

A glimpse of my nine-year-old self alone in the house passed in my thoughts. I had snuck a look through the fancy scope and saw Audra Schultz, Mother's friend who lived a mile away, walking around her kitchen in her underwear, as clearly as if she were in the room with me. I thought that in my eagerness to peer through the apparatus, I had moved it, changed its focus away from the moon he'd assigned my brothers to study. If my father noticed, he didn't reprimand me. He never scolded me. I was his favorite.

"Spy, huh? Did he tell you that?" the woman asked, her hand on my shoulder, lightly.

"No. It took a long time and a lot of research, but I finally put together enough facts to figure it out. About a year ago. After that, I never asked him because I knew he wasn't allowed to tell."

He had died alone at his apartment, a place so neat it could have been a motel room. The cleaning woman found him. Heart attack, the Medical Examiner said. Afterward, I found not a single shred of personal data, other than his driver's license, in the entire place. Nothing. Surely that was just as he'd been trained. All his other identities had been destroyed or well hidden.

His clothes hung neatly in the closet, underwear folded in the dresser. A stack of library books on computer programming, digital photography, and one about development of the Internet, occupied the nightstand. The gun I remembered he had, a thirty-eight caliber police special, he'd called it, was not there. That surprised me, but he'd probably had to turn it in when he retired. His billfold contained only the license and a photo of the three of us as children. No mail on the counter. No food in the refrigerator; only a box of wine. No money. That didn't surprise me. He would have worked off the books, and probably had a safe deposit box somewhere stuffed with large bills. Hated paying taxes.

The woman spoke again, and I turned toward her. It never hurt to be polite.

"Well, if he had told you, he could have made you believe it. The man was as full of shit as a Christmas turkey." The woman laughed, a brief, strangled sound. "Reese could be charming when he wanted to. Lots of women fell for it, too."

"Did you?" I wondered at myself as soon as I asked. I had suspected, but never had proof about other women. Mother never said; there was a lot she never said.

"Oh sure, but not like some women. I was your mother's friend. I never slept with him."

If it wouldn't have been improper at an occasion like this, I would have pointed out that a secret agent establishes a cover and remains true to it—it's in all the books. The "philandering husband" was a perfect cover story that explained everything. For example, his long absences from home. Mother must have known when he went away on assignments; she never complained to us when he left, and whenever he returned, she never raised her voice to him.

I didn't even try to be subtle when I checked my watch again. Eight o'clock. When this was over, I still had to write the eulogy. My brothers said that I should be the one to speak and had pressed me to agree. Kent said he "was sure he would choke up" and Tommy reminded me how well I had done Mother's. Of course I had; neither one of them bothered to show up at all until the service.

The only minister whose name any of us knew was the pastor of the thousand-member evangelical church Kent's wife attends. No way any of us would give him the chance to preach. We didn't discuss that as a possibility. So, for our father's funeral, by default and for an additional fee, the funeral director would handle the service and I would read the eulogy. And I still had no clue what I would say.

Exposing him now, for what he really was, seemed disloyal, or at the very least, potentially dangerous. Besides, even people accustomed to slight exaggerations lauding the recently dead would likely scoff at the idea of his being involved in clandestine activities on behalf of his country. How, in a eulogy, would I convince them? I had only the results of the research I had dedicated myself to for years. No official agency had come forth to acknowledge him, thus supporting my conclusion. Those in deep cover lived alone, even when they were with others. And they always died alone.

Watching the woman's profile, I could tell she was intentionally observing every person in the room. Then she turned toward me again. Something told me she was satisfied it was safe to stay a bit longer. She said, "Tell me what makes you think he was a secret agent."

I bit the inside of my cheek and looked away. Vivaldi's "Four Seasons" continued in the background, apparently free of charge. We hadn't requested music for this visitation.

Why try to explain to this woman? She obviously hadn't liked him. Then it struck me; she could be an operative too, tying up loose ends, sent to execute anyone who could out him, even after his death. I stood, as if I had forgotten something I was to do. How stupid. She'd never do anything to me here. I sat again, one chair farther from her.

Tommy appeared near my right elbow. "Glass of red? Not the best, but not bad." He offered me a half-filled glass. I took my time sipping and feeling the warm trickle creep down my throat.

Introductions would be appropriate, but the woman's name was a mystery. I said, "Tommy, this is one of Mother's friends." Then looking back at the woman, "This is my brother, Tommy. Maybe you two remember each other."

"Sorry to say I don't," he said. Then Tommy smiled our father's smile, the one always accompanied by a wink, as if he shared a secret with the recipient.

She looked up at him. "Marta." She raised the eyebrow again and peered at Tommy. "Yes, you're definitely his son. I'd recognize the smile anywhere," the woman said.

"Not necessarily a compliment in my books," Tommy said. He set his glass down and looked briefly toward the casket. "You were right, Sis. Those are beautiful flowers." He glanced at Marta briefly, then retrieved his glass. "Sorry. Didn't mean to be rude. Nice to meet you." He headed out of the room, glass in hand.

Eight forty-five, a quick glance at my watch told me. Marta, if that was her real name, hadn't moved from her chair. Apparently, her mission required that she stay. I said, "I really should speak to some of the others."

"Sure, I'll wait here."

I shivered slightly in the draft from a ceiling fan as I crossed the room toward the caterer's serving station. Three men, each about seventy, my father's age, huddled near the bar. Two of them busied themselves getting their glasses filled. As I reached the bar, I heard the third man say, "Fellows, I believe this is his daughter." Each of them offered a handshake and a name I didn't bother to try to remember.

I didn't recognize any of them. "Thank you for being here. We appreciate it," I said. All three nodded. "Did you work with my father?" Maybe they could fill in some facts to support my research.

"Uh huh, radio station in Sweetwater," one of them said. "He took the overnight shift, out at the transmitter shack, the only one of us with a license."

I remembered how hysterically I screamed and cried when, just after my fourteenth birthday, Mother said we were moving to Sweetwater to live with him. This man's statement verified that my father had been there. He'd left Sweetwater, had come back home. We kids and mother never moved. I hadn't understood at the time.

One of the others stared into his empty glass, and spoke without looking at me. He said, "We worked together at the Record News in Wichita Falls for a while. He was a photographer, crime beat mostly. I worked editorial. Hell of a guy. Lots of fun. Back before he married."

That sort of job would have been one of the reasons the Agency would have chosen him—his interest in crime and intrigue, working odd hours, professional skill. Yes, it fit.

The third, a short, rotund, grizzled fellow said, "He ran the recording equipment on some offshore geophysical boats in the Gulf. I was Party Chief on those runs. Back in the fifties. You were just a little tyke then, lived up in Monroe, Louisiana, if I recall."

Mother had never mentioned that we lived in Louisiana. But I knew from all I'd read that a spy's colleagues would all have their own covers. And would never betray my father's, no matter how far in the distant past. I felt myself relax.

I looked at the doorway, and considered slipping out quietly without a word to anyone. How wrong would it be to leave your own father's visitation? I'd need a cover story. Or maybe I wouldn't. Let Kent entertain his employees. His wife could write the caterer a check.

Nine o'clock. Surely, anyone else who was coming would appear in the next few minutes. Who visits at a funeral home at nine in the evening? I paced, feeling I was trudging, toward the opposite wall, away from the group consuming canapés and wine and trading stories of their various old days, each one carefully true to his legend.

I made my way across the sound-muffling carpet, then around the room's outer boundary, passing the casket, the flowers, the overstuffed chairs. My circuit of the room ended when I returned to where Marta still sat. I couldn't be rude. She might actually have been Mother's friend, not a spy. Although I knew doing it posed a risk—who knew what she had in that large leopard print tote she hauled in—I returned to the chair one space away from her.

Before I was even seated, she said, "Tell me more about Reese being a spy."

"I will. But it has to be confidential." I hesitated just long enough to imply caution, then cleared my throat and looked around. (I have some skills myself, acting being one of them.) "I wouldn't want to bore you with things you already know. So, if you'll remind me how and when you knew my parents, I'll begin from there."

The woman leaned close and cut her eyes toward me. "Sure. Reese and my first husband, John, both worked for Nationwide Geotechnical, back in the late forties. The five men on the crew and we two wives, we all lived like a bunch of gypsies in little trailers all over West Texas. Surveying for oil. John was Party Chief; there was a land man, a driller, a jug hustler who handled the dynamite, and Reese. He ran the electronics in the recording truck.

"They'd park the four trailers—the jug hustler and the driller shared one—in some dinky trailer park in dry little towns like Iraan or Big Lake and take off, leaving the two of us for days at a time while they did whatever it was they did. Then they'd be back and we'd all drink and party and then the same thing over again the next week. Went on like that for a few weeks and then off we'd go to the next little burg." She shook her head once and laughed, a single snort, as if the story she was telling was a bad joke—too long, no punch line.

"Did you actually see the work they did?" According to the books I'd read, even back then there were clandestine jobs no one would ever know the truth about.

Marta shook her head. "Nah. But your mother and I—neither of us more than twenty—got to be close. No television in those days. Just the radio and our magazines. And lots of talk. Once a month, after payday, we'd go to the nearest town and shop, someplace like Hobbs or Odessa, didn't matter where, all those oilfield towns smelled alike—refinery gas. The smell of money, everyone was fond of saying. They never gave us much money so it was mostly window shopping.

"We told each other everything, from why our husbands hadn't been drafted to how they slapped us around when they got drunk, which was every Saturday night. Don't get me wrong, we probably deserved it. Probably started most of the fights we got the worst of. I know I did."

A bit of calmness crept over me, took the edge off my wariness. This woman was no spy. If she was, she was asking for trouble. One of the rules was, "never tell elaborate lies, only what is absolutely necessary and then, build it around the truth." Her story was far too specific. It had to be true, even if Mother never had mentioned it. I said, "All that was before I was born."

"Your folks left the crew when your mom got pregnant with your older brother. But we kept in touch right up until she died." The woman stopped speaking and leaned close, touched me on the shoulder again. "Honey, you don't have to tell me anything you don't want to. Your mother told me how crazy you always were about him. It's just that you look so much like your mother I felt we could talk."

"You think I look like her?"

"Carbon copy."

I searched for my wineglass under my chair, took a long drink, and waited for the warmth. After a deep breath, I said, "Thank you for understanding. And for telling me about my mother."

The woman stood. "If you've found something that proved your dad was a spy, well I hope she knew, too. For her sake." I watched her take a long look at the three men at the bar. She said, "I'll be going now." She patted my hand one last time.

I sipped my wine and watched her leave. I still had a eulogy to write.

Nine-thirty. It looked like the old guys were going to stay until the caterer closed down. They hadn't moved. And four of Kent's people remained. Tommy caught my eye. I took another deep breath, squared my shoulders and walked to where Kent stood listening to the praise of his salespeople. I whispered to his wife, who stood beside him, gazing at something that might be a hundred miles away. "I'm going now. I have a eulogy to write. Tell Kent I'll see him at the service." His wife's expression remained blank as she nodded, a single bob of her head.

As I passed Tommy and the old spies, I said to him, "See you at my apartment." I doubted he'd make it tonight.

A calmness I hadn't felt all evening settled on me. Putting the eulogy together shouldn't be that tricky now—only a matter of assembling pieces from material in my files, if I focused on the task.

Five years ago, after Mother died, when our father dropped from sight, I began writing accounts of my own memories and notes on anything either of my brothers mentioned involving him. At the time, I had wanted to recall as much as possible because I feared he was gone for good. I hadn't had the chance to say goodbye.

The more data I collected, the more I suspected that nothing was as I had thought for all those years. His work, his absences, every bit of it showed a pattern, consistently inconsistent, as I looked at it spread out on the pages of notes. Developing data displays, a technique often used by those who study chaos theory, became a fascination of mine.

My father had been an intermittent presence, making our lives seem as if they were lived within an unpredictable weather cycle. Occasional temperate periods were disrupted by months-long heat inversions, sunny calm weeks receded abruptly when Hurricane Reese blew back into town.

When I was eight or ten, a news story about a man with wives and children in two separate cities set me wondering if I had a half-sister in some exotic location, Denver maybe. But now, as an adult, since I connected all the evidence, it had become clear. He was a secret agent. I had been wrong to wish each time that he left, that he would never return. I should have been worried for his safety. How could I put what I knew into a proper eulogy?

After he turned up again, two years ago, saying he'd retired, I saw him often. He spent hours in the library where I work, reading in the non-fiction stacks. And we had lunch or dinner together at least twice a month. I never asked what he did with the rest of his time.

Our conversations often reminded me of chat between people on public transportation. I didn't mind because by then I suspected that little of his past could ever be public. It pleased me that, unlike Mother, he didn't seem concerned that I had never married, that my work occupied all my time.

When he didn't appear at the reference desk to greet me this past Monday, I suspected he'd left again, one final assignment. Then Tuesday, the apartment manager called, saying he didn't have my name, but that my number had been listed as the emergency contact.

And so there I was, at ten p.m., the night before the funeral, sitting at the desk in my study, trying to write a final tribute. The door to this room stayed locked when Tommy visited. I didn't want to have to explain. It had become my research lab. The array of files, color coded and cross referenced, housed in a lockable fire safe, attested to my thorough work. Thirty-six books—on spycraft, history of U.S. Intelligence operations, and spy-related novels—all arranged according to their LC numbers, lined two bookshelves. A couple of months ago, I'd outlined a plan to computerize all my data, for backup purposes.

I chose one of several notes, at random, from the first file I took from the metal case. It described his sleep pattern— nine specific memories that showed him asleep in the daytime on the living room couch, or sitting cross-legged in bed, reading all night. A footnote mentioned Mother sleeping with a pillow covering her head. No better pattern for a spy—alert while the rest of the world slept.

Another sheet from the same file summarized his long absences from home. Over the course of the twelve years I could recall, he'd been gone at least ten times, for a month or longer. My analysis evaluated the difference in the atmosphere at home during those times. "I remember feeling relief each time he left and dread each time he returned—chaos would reign once more." That was one of my earliest entries, before I had enough data.

I smiled, as I had when I remembered the incident, reading my report of his having tapped the phone in the appliance store he operated. A local solid citizen's frequent requests to use the phone prompted him to install the bug. Over a two-month period, he recorded several hours of breathless exchanges between the citizen and the wife of a local Baptist deacon. Mother and I had laughed aloud at "Are you wearing any underwear?" and "Tell me what you intend to do to me next time" and other lines that even to my teenage ears had sounded like dialogue from a bad movie.

Another entire file contained recollections of his various electronic interests. Shortwave radio equipment filled a room next to the den. Many nights I fell asleep annoyed by the static and drone of single-sideband signals from Australia, Pacific Islands, and South America. He'd explained that nights provided the best reception, greatest possibility of distance. And the QSL cards he posted on a bulletin board from those people were "like greeting cards," he'd said, "just for fun." At the time it seemed plausible. Some nights he tapped out Morse code messages, to people who didn't speak English, he'd said. Dah-dah-dit-dah all night. A hobby. Now I knew it was more.

I shuffled the files and found the one that listed his jobs. The ones I'd heard tonight about the geophysical crews and the newspaper photography weren't there. I couldn't stop myself from updating the file, adding them to the list that included appliance store manager, television weatherman (late night), inventor (a list of his several never-patented inventions followed), radio station owner, airplane autopilot installer, lounge operator, and sales (a long list different sales jobs from appliances to school textbooks to x-ray equipment followed).

I avoided opening the thick folder that held notes on each of the spy novels I had read. Ludlum, Fleming, LeCarre, and several others' work had provided details, all displayed in a spreadsheet that extended over two pages taped together lengthwise. (Tasks for my next project included converting that spreadsheet into an Excel format.) Their fiction had guided my tour of the memories of my childhood and convinced me even further.

I lifted out the only black folder in the box—my conclusions. I scanned to the final paragraph, which I read slowly, considering how I might use it as part of the eulogy. "A spy has to maintain all kinds of cover—family, work record, personal habits, friends and contacts, daily routines. Living in a small town made developing a convincing cover difficult. He succeeded by creating one that showed him as a man who was multi-skilled, restless, and who had a roving eye."

I pictured my brothers' reactions if I were to read that. And Kent's wife and Marta—all I could imagine were faces filled with pity, for me. I straightened the papers and closed the file, replaced it in the organizer.

If only I had one piece of hard evidence, I could surely make my case, at least strongly enough to make Tommy doubt his own warped view. No time for that now. A eulogy demanded to be written. And spoken.

The last aspect of our father's cover on which I had made notes involved interpersonal behavior. I didn't open the dark blue folder reserved for those. I preferred to recall the man laughing, telling a joke, smiling the smile that Tommy now owned. The other things—call them traits or habits—him shouting at Mother in the middle of the night, berating his brother Clint for enjoying a simple rural life, cursing anyone who disagreed with him, stumbling home drunk, lying on the couch issuing orders, disrupting any semblance of normal routine by missing meals and cancelling plans—I intended to forget.

At two a.m., I put the final period on what amounted to a hagiographic account of our father. It told of a self-educated, multi-talented man whose influences had been vast and his many good works conducted anonymously. I hoped no one would recognize it as a parody of all eulogies I had ever sat through. It would have to do.

The small funeral chapel dwarfs the handful of people attending the ceremony. The funeral home personnel; Kent and his family; Tommy, who arrived just as the recording of "Amazing Grace" began playing; a woman who seems to be with Tommy; the three older men with the appetites for hors d'oeuvres; four men and two women, probably connected to Kent's company, cluster in the first three rows of pews. Marta sits, like an extra digit, separately in the fourth row.

Following two other hymns, the funeral director reads the obituary, a terse paragraph giving vital statistics only. Then he prays a nearly interminable prayer. And finally, he sits. That's my cue to step to the podium. I clear my throat and breathe deeply. I lift the typed pages, raise my eyes and fix on Tommy's face, then Kent's. Both blank as hired mourners'.

I drop the paper back to the podium. Then I walk across the small stage to the casket, next to the arrangement of birds of paradise. I pass my hand over the flawless wood of the casket lid, and rap against it with my knuckles, once, a bass note that raises my brothers' eyes toward me. After a moment, while I survey each face in the audience, I speak.

"Each person here today knew Reese Murray differently— some when he was young, other as he aged—some as friends, others as family. Each of us would describe him differently. For that reason, I ask that you now consider how you might pay tribute to him, if you were standing here instead of me. I will be silent for two minutes as we each do that."

I return to the podium and for the full two minutes I stand with my head bowed, following my watch as it counts the seconds. I hear sniffling from the fourth row. Those minutes should have given me an opportunity to review my script. Instead I remembered the many times I had complained that eulogies most often were hypocritical efforts to try to trick God into believing the departed was a saint, regardless of how vile a sinner he might have been. Or if the person delivering the eulogy actually believed the catalogue of sterling qualities she recited, then she was afflicted by incurable naiveté.

After the two minutes pass, I look again at the page of notes, then fold the paper three times into a rectangle and slide it into my pocket.

I raise my head and glance at Kent, who stares into his lap. Tommy returns my gaze. I speak slowly and distinctly. "I heard my older brother describe our father as a unique individual, always ahead of his time, and probably misplaced in the small town where he grew up. I could not have said it better. My brothers and I know that he loved us very much, in his way. And we also know he left something in each of us that helped make us who we are. Our lives will be changed by his absence."

I nod to the funeral director, who jerks to attention, dropping his copy of the program for the service. "Amazing Grace" plays again. Walking slowly, attending to the hymn's tempo, I return to my seat behind the podium. Then I allow myself to exhale, so gently no one can hear. No one can fault my performance. I told the truth and I hadn't blown his cover.

Between Us

One hundred seventeen. Another record! Until now, the greatest number of new emails for a single day on her Gia Caraway fan site had been sixty-nine. That was three years ago when her third book came out. The writer, subject of the fans' interest, wasn't the only one who kept up with the numbers. Her editor had administrative access to her website and could see the incoming mail and Jean's responses. Occasionally the editor furnished Jean, who used the pseudonym Gia, a report that showed the number of views of her website correlated with sales of her print and e-books. Website views demonstrated a weakly positive correlation with sales. Fan e-mail numbers correlated strongly with sales.

Plus, now that Jean's publisher supplied a person to tend to her social media presence, the reports also contained far more than she cared to know about the number of page views, likes, and followers for her author pages and/or her books on Facebook, Pinterest, Goodreads, Amazon, Instagram, and Twitter. For all she knew, her editor, Audra Camp, could also document a running inventory of the contents of Jean's underwear drawer.

What Audra didn't know was that Jean was as much a fabrication as Gia. Johnnie Lyn Berry had created Jean Barlow just as surely as she had birthed Gia Caraway. Jean dealt with the editor, signed contracts, owned a telephone and a bank account of her own, had a g-mail address and a social security number, and employed her own accountant. Gia, whose name stood in bold print on more than 400,000 copies of paperbacks and electronic books, had no time for those details. She lived an exciting life that her fans were certain was the source of the erotic, romantic escapades her heroines enjoyed.

If Johnnie Lyn hadn't done another smart thing in her life, deciding to create Jean qualified. Johnnie Lyn thought of Jean as the buffer who represented her in the world of romance fiction. Since the amazing numbers of sales of her first book with the publisher, Jean had complied with all of Audra's wishes, accepted all her guidance. Audra used the words "guiding your career development." Jean thought about Trilby and Svengali.

So far, the only disagreement between her and her editor had been about having a social media person at the publishing house respond to her fan mail. Jean preferred to do that herself. She didn't mind that the avatar they'd created for her communicated on Facebook like a twenty-two year old from Brooklyn, OMG! If that's what the company thought would sell her brand, it was fine with her. But people who went to the trouble to write fan mail deserved a personal answer—from Gia.

So here she was, at nine o'clock on a perfectly beautiful Monday evening in June, 2011, sitting in her writing room, dealing with fan mail. She should be outside enjoying the West Texas sunset. The first one she opened said, "Dear Gia, I'm sixty-two this year and have read every one of your books since the first. You've outdone yourself with this eleventh one. I love that you're telling MY story without our ever having met. I don't know how you do it, but it's clear to me that somehow you know about the adventures I had in my earlier days. I often said I should write an autobiography. Thanks to you, honey, I don't need to. Keep up the good work. Your fan always, Carla in Ft. Worth."

This wasn't the first fan who was certain she was the subject of Gia's novels. Her template file held a response which she quickly personalized, assuring Carla in Ft. Worth that it was all fiction and congratulating her on having led such an interesting life.

The next email in the queue replaced Jean's smile with a wrinkle between her eyebrows. Not fan mail, it was from Audra, who usually wrote to her Jean Barlow email address, or just called Jean's phone. (Gia didn't have a phone.) This email, here in Gia's fan mail, was flagged High Priority—in red letters.

It didn't even begin with Audra's usual gushy greeting Dearest Jean, my star of stars. This one opened with Jean, This is important for both of us.

Jean scanned the first paragraph. Her publishing company had wangled a spot on the program at a romance fiction conference coming up in San Antonio in September. It was to be a huge event, bringing together fans and authors—presentations for writers on the first day, the next day open to fans, also. THINK STAR TREK CONVENTION! THINK SALES OPPORTUNITIES!! Audra had been assigned, as Editorial Director of Body Heat, the company's line of erotic romances, to make a major presentation.

Gia didn't attend conferences and neither did Jean, ever. Audra knew that. Jean scrolled quickly and then she saw the punch line. You and I will co-star as the conference keynoters. I've attached an outline. I assume you will be as thrilled as I am with this opportunity and will be eager to join me. But I must have a formal, written answer from you no later than end of business on Friday, June17.

Johnnie Lyn heard a sound like a balloon deflating, then realized she was the source. She pushed back from the computer and stood, staring at the letter on the screen. Then she sat again, closed the email, and powered off the computer. Her mother's face, sad and disappointed, flashed into her mind and immediately after, a burning sensation rose from her stomach toward her throat.

The largest meetings she'd attended in years were English Department faculty meetings at Red River Regional Community College. She'd quit there nearly five years ago. Johnnie Lyn did not attend conferences, and since she quit going to church when she was twenty-one, seldom ventured into any group. But Jean—what would Jean do?

Certainly, she did things Johnnie Lyn didn't dare. First, she'd bullied her way into having a wardrobe of her own. Not an extensive selection, but she'd whispered that a girl needed work clothes. The next day she ordered from Frederick's online. Then she'd said, "If you won't get a haircut so we don't look like a Holiness preacher's daughter, then I must have a wig. Something thick and wavy, the kind that makes men want to grab a handful. I was born to be a brunette, not this drab beige you insist on leaving natural. Can't you see the gray starting at the temples?"

Any time Johnnie Lyn wanted a lift, all she had to do was let Jean start talking to her. Or if she wanted to laugh, remembering the day Jean was born always did the trick. Even though it had been more than four years, she remembered the whole thing clearly. Far in advance, she had every detail listed, from the steps necessary to get the official legal change of name all the way to finally handing a Denton, Texas, banker a cashier's check to open Jean's first bank account. She'd spent weeks preparing, thinking all along it was probably the closest she'd ever get to feeling mother-to-be anticipation.

Her stomach grumbled, told her she'd overlooked eating supper. She had no trouble deciding on oatmeal, quick and easy. Its cinnamony aroma briefly distracted her from rerunning the "birth of Jean" memory. With the steaming bowl on a plate, along with an English muffin and a glass of milk, she sat at the kitchen table. Warm oatmeal reminded her of all that was good about childhood. She took her time buttering the muffin and thought again of Jean's arrival.

Johnnie Lyn had known all her planning was a gamble. Maybe the publishing company wouldn't accept her proposal for a series. Her previous, minor success with two self-published "tame" romances wouldn't necessarily convince the editor she could write the steamier material the new imprint, Body Heat, promised. But on the chance that they would, Jean (not yet a legal person, but....) submitted three sample chapters.

A month later, the phone rang. In response to Johnnie Lyn's cautious hello, a female voice said, "This is Audra Camp at Body Heat. Calling for Jean Barlow." The silent seconds that ticked by while Johnnie Lyn comprehended what she'd heard must have stretched longer than it seemed. The voice claiming to be the editor said, "Hello, hello. Is anyone there?"

That same afternoon, Johnnie Lyn drove to Denton, a manila file beside her holding the required fingerprints and the official State of Texas form petitioning for legal change of name, complete except for her signature which must be affixed before a notary. The following afternoon, after a day of paperwork and legal details, the attorney said, "That's it. All the forms are approved." She shook Johnnie Lyn's hand. "I'll see that the change is recorded in the Denton County Clerk's office within a week. But starting right now, you can enjoy your life as Jean Barlow."

With any news, the first person she called was always her mother. But not that time. Mother would never understand and would probably be hurt. Instead, Johnnie Lyn drove back to Wichita Falls, letting herself feel like Jean for a little while. Then when she passed through Henrietta and soon saw the edge of Wichita Falls, she said aloud, "I'm proud of you, Jean. Now we have a secret. Women need to have secrets." Before long she parked in the garage of her duplex and felt the same as usual, a girl who grew up in Archer City and had never gotten far from there.

After putting her dishes in the sink, she opened the refrigerator to put away the butter. Fifteen minutes went by as she emptied the vegetable crisper drawer and the shelves, washed and dried them, then replaced the food, and stood staring in the cool space. Making the short trip to her computer, Johnnie Lyn waited for courage and hoped for the correct answer to Audra's email to come to her, preferably to spring from her brow like Athena, fully formed. After staring at Audra's email for several minutes, Jean typed a response saying she would answer by Friday.

Her mother would have said that was putting off the devil, something she repeatedly had warned Johnnie Lyn against. "Face up to problems. Deal with them. If you don't, they grow. Take my word for it."

She'd heard that plenty of times and filed it in the same mental category as "eat all your vegetables or you won't grow." Only after she was sixteen and her mother confessed (that was the word she'd used) her teenaged, hidden, unwed pregnancy that resulted in her only child's birth did Johnnie Lyn understand the code in that warning. She promptly stopped complaining about her mother's making her attend church. She even discarded the jeans from her wardrobe and let her hair grow, all according to church rules. Her grades topped every class. She graduated as valedictorian and virgin. But she never quite overcame a tendency to procrastinate.

Occupied by staring unfocused past the computer screen and through the window beyond, Johnnie Lyn told herself to get rational. Make a decision, then act. She opened the MS Word file that held the manuscript of the current romance novel, half finished, far ahead of deadline. Then she closed the file. Jean wouldn't like it if she tried to work in her place.

The computer's reminder tone sounded. She didn't need to focus to know the message said, "Call Mom." They were in touch at least twice daily. She was usually the one who made the calls or sent the first email—morning and evening. It was the least she could do; her mother had sacrificed for her. A truly good daughter would drive the twenty-six miles from Wichita Falls to Archer City more often than once a month.

After the usual greetings, Johnnie Lyn volunteered a fabricated account of a busy day grading student papers and preparing lectures. If she described her day first, she seldom had to respond to any questions. She'd developed a story line some time back, based on what had been fact pre-Body Heat—she taught English Composition to freshman students for the regional community college three evenings per week; she enjoyed the work; and most of her students were adults returning to school, not typical freshmen. So today she said, "You won't believe what one of them did this time. In purple ink, he wrote on his paper that he had done all the research for the assignment and had it on stored on a flash drive, which he wore on his wrist, but then it fell off into the commode and he flushed it. The last sentence said, 'So may I please have an extension on the deadline?'"

Her mother, a young fifty-nine, usually laughed readily. Tonight, her only reaction was, "People always want to get away with whatever they can, I suppose."

"Are you feeling okay, Mom?"

"Oh, yes. I'm just kind of preoccupied."

"You didn't forget to eat supper did you?"

"Ha! You know I seldom miss a meal."

"That makes two of us." Johnnie Lyn said. Then she paused, giving her mother an opening if she wanted it. After several silent seconds while she listened to her mother breathe, she said, "The things on your mind, anything I can help with?"

Her mother's next breath sounded like a sigh. Then she said, "Will you be coming out this week? It's been three weeks. Maybe Thursday or Friday?"

Thinking of Audra's deadline, Johnnie Lyn said, "Thursday's probably best for me."

"Good. We can talk then. I'll cook supper."

"It's a date. I'll be there around five and I'll bring dessert. Anything else?"

"No. You have a good night, honey. Love you."

"You, too, Mom."

Johnnie Lyn stared at the phone's screen after she closed the call. Now this. All these years her mother had believed her daughter was living a happily single life, using her college education, doing some good in the world. At least, that's what Johnnie Lyn believed—her mother never asked questions or made comments suggesting she doubted her.

That perfect daughter would never be able explain that she hadn't taught a class in more than four years, that she wrote the paperback books that girls hid from their mothers, and that mothers hid under their mattresses until their husbands went on fishing trips. As far as her pious mother was concerned, there was no excuse for lying, ever. She'd never questioned Johnnie Lyn about why she didn't attend church any more. But in other ways—the long-sleeved blouses, long complicated hairdo, and lack of obvious makeup—Johnnie Lyn let her mother know her girl hadn't strayed far. She had no reason to doubt the story of her daughter's life, the lies she'd spun into whole cloth.

Not so far, at least. But at least twice since she took her new name, she'd had to lie to other people. In high school, she'd been forgettable in every way, except for her grades. And wouldn't you know, the person she'd beaten to be class valedictorian saw her at the mall. Thank goodness, that day she'd been dressed in Jean's slacks, wig, and makeup. Her classmate had said, "Don't I know you? Maybe from high school?"

Maybe it was the wig and the makeup that made Jean, not Johnnie Lyn answer, but the perfect reply came out without a thought. She'd offered a sweet smile and said, "I don't think so. I went to school in Henrietta. Did you?"

The second time had been a closer call. Ordinarily Johnnie Lyn shopped for groceries late at night and saw few people other than the employees stocking the shelves. But one afternoon, she needed green chiles for a stew. A woman who had been two years below her in school reported to her mother in Archer City that she'd seen, "that smart girl, the one who didn't wear makeup, but when I told her we went to school together in Archer City, she said her name was Jean and she was from Amarillo, just passing through." The mother had repeated this to Johnnie Lyn's mother, who then passed it along to Johnnie Lyn in an email with the comment—"I thought you'd get a laugh out of this. I can assure you, you do not have a twin."

Each of those times, for days afterward, dreams woke Johnnie Lyn, and each of those included a scene in which a twelve-year-old version of her stood before a church congregation and asked forgiveness for the sin of lying. She lived in dread of seeing pain and disappointment on her mother's face. Worse yet was the very real possibility that her mother would follow her church's rules and shun her, sever all contact.

Even when she was fully awake, any way she might think of to try to explain changing her name and telling years of lies to her mother, it would always come out sounding like a betrayal. Now the day she'd dreaded had arrived. Thursday was the day she'd have to explain. She dropped the phone and closed her eyes, leaning back in her desk chair.

Jean's voice said, "Oh please, get over yourself. You have gone through this drama more times than I care to count. Every time she says, 'We need to talk,' you get all lathered up." Johnnie Lyn opened her eyes. Jean was right. "And never yet has she ever said a word about me or about your skulking through life worrying what people think. She doesn't know."

Johnnie Lyn stood and nodded. Jean was far more rational than she ever could be. But still, what sort of ungrateful person changes her name, writes what some would call filth, and builds a fabric of lies about her work and life? An ungrateful person. That's who. She hoped Jean couldn't read her mind.

"Think about this. Why shouldn't I be on that panel? I'm the best Body Heat has to offer." Jean got this way. Once she started, she was hard to shut up. "No one at that meeting would ever mistake me for you, much less call me Johnnie Lyn."

Johnnie Lyn's voice, softer and more tentative than Jean's, interrupted, "What about that woman from Dalhart who writes those Christian romances? I recognized her picture on a book jacket. She and I were at church camp in eighth grade. I'm sure she'll be there."

"We'll need to get my wig done, unless you're willing to get about a yard of that mane of yours cut off and have the gray colored. Maybe we could go with highlights." Jean paused briefly. "You don't have to decide right this minute, but you'll see, a good haircut and color will make you feel like a different woman. Just think, San Antonio, the Riverwalk, mariachis." She stopped talking only long enough to take a breath, then pushed on. "I wish you drank. I could use a glass or two of wine right now."

Tuesday morning, sunlight stabbed at Johnnie Lyn's left hand, then traced a line across her arm, arriving seconds later smack in the middle of her left eyelid. She rolled away but now she was awake and had no choice but to get up. Even though it was only six o'clock, she attacked her usual Tuesday routine as if she were under scrutiny. First she checked in with her mother by email. As usual, they exchanged a brief chatty couple of sentences and wishes for a good day. After that, besides vacuuming every room, dusting—there was always dust in this part of Texas, and cleaning the bathroom fixtures, her scurrying included a trip to have her five-year-old Chevy Malibu's oil changed.

She thought about treating herself to lunch out while her car was serviced, but the quick-lube franchise actually did finish in ten minutes, so she took that as a sign she should just go ahead and buy groceries, get home, and put her week's worth of meals on to cook. Then she'd eat and rest a bit before she went to work. All morning, she didn't have a free second to think. And any time Jean made a peep, Johnnie Lyn ignored her. Days like this, when everything moved smoothly, she congratulated herself on the joys of living alone.

Her usual work day began at three in the afternoon and ended at eleven, with thirty minutes off for supper. Working at home made dawdling attractive; the Internet made the dawdling seem somewhat more than wasting time, if you called browsing and occasionally printing out a Wiki entry research. She figured out a long time ago that the only way to assure she never missed a deadline was to create order in her life. So, each weekday afternoon, she changed from whatever she had on and dressed for work, went to her writing room, and began by reading and editing the pages she'd written the prior day.

Tuesday, Jean took over as soon as Johnnie Lyn opened the closet to select the day's clothing. After a quick shower, she situated her wig and gave it a brisk comb-through. Makeup took a while. She felt like doing sultry eyes that day. That meant three shades of green to bring out her hazel, liner, kohl accents, then mascara base and a final coat of black. No false lashes for her— she'd been blessed with triple rows top and bottom. She leaned back from the magnifying mirror and blinked rapidly. Satisfied, she quickly applied a very thin base followed by brushed-on blush that emphasized her cheekbones. Then she selected lipstick, true red, and expertly applied a perfect pout, enlarging the upper lip just a millimeter beyond its border. The silver studs of her earrings attached to tiny black feathers that brushed against her neck with each movement.

At three o'clock on the dot, wearing black crotchless panties, a zebra striped satin bra with heart-shaped nipple-peek cutouts, sleek black yoga pants, and a tasteful black tunic suitable for opening the front door if an emergency arose, she sat at her computer. Her feet were bare. Her red, five-inch-stiletto pumps lay on the bed, just in case. While the machine ran through its start-up menu, she leaned to her left and lit the sandalwood scented candle. Its light flickered against the closed wooden blinds, making the room a dusky oasis in a glaring desert of a Texas summer day.

Setting the mood this way hadn't occurred to Johnnie Lyn, but Jean saw the need immediately the first time she read a fan letter she called her all time favorite. *I can never thank you enough for "Opening Night in Texas." It definitely opened me. I can't say which passage in particular made things right for me, but I will tell you that I read the book all in one night, here alone in my apartment. There's a bright red star on my calendar on that date. It marks the first orgasm I ever experienced! Did I mention THANK YOU? Signed, a happy thirty-year old. p.s. I wore out that first copy and had to buy a second.*

Johnnie Lyn had never admitted anything about her romance writing to her previous supervisor in the English Department at the community college. Only academic publications or fiction published in forms other than mass market paperback were worthy of "counting" toward retention and promotion. Completing the documents for her annual review her second year, the blank space under the heading "Publications" reminded her she'd never be promoted in that job. Then she noticed that the "Community Service" category had equal weight in the fancy formula used to justify the promotion decisions. Service was a valuable faculty enterprise. So Jean suggested that improving the lives of lonely women, as documented by this fan letter, should be included in her evaluation portfolio. Johnnie Lyn had promised to consider the suggestion.

Jean worked rapidly, easily describing the scenes she imagined. Her printed plot outline lay on the desk beside the computer, but she seldom consulted it. The heroine of *Two Tickets to the Fireman's Ball* let her yearning be known from page one. She wanted a man who would notice her, treasure her, and make passionate love to her until she was senseless, unlike her real-life, football coach husband. They lived in a small town in Texas. By page six, Jean had made evident that this woman had to get out of town and get a different man if her wants and needs would ever be satisfied. Next she complicated things by having this lonely wife feel committed to the idea that her marriage must be maintained and that no one must know about her lusty yearnings. And then, Jean set the stage for trouble by sending her character to an out-of-town, week-long meeting of . . . (she'd fill in that blank later) in (decide on the town later).

Jean wrote fast, leaving occasional blanks in favor of getting the action on the page. She'd fill them and polish it all in revision. She stopped long enough to eat, and then rushed back to work. Next, came the part she liked best. Leaning back in the desk chair, her eyes closed, she moved her fingertips slowly across her nipples, already made sensitive and erect by scenes she saw behind her closed lids. She opened her eyes, and sat upright. A flurry of keystrokes, interrupted by brief pauses, creating a rhythm that continued for several minutes. Her breathing accelerated as she worked, then she paused and relaxed against the chair. She read what she'd completed.

Neither of them spoke in the glass elevator, but he stood close to Monica as the lobby shrank away and the transparent capsule transported them toward the Concierge level on the thirtieth floor. The raincoat draped over his left arm covered his hand as it slid from her waist downward. Reaching her left buttock, he pressed lightly against her firm flesh with each finger, one at a time. She managed to stand perfectly still, but shifted her eyes to meet his glance and see the slightest hint of a smile flit across his lips. The other passenger exited on fifteen. As the door closed behind him, Eliot said, "I hope you don't mind. I ordered Champagne. You look like a woman who deserves the best."

She worked to control her breathing. More alcohol could be a mistake after the wine at dinner. But Champagne was worth taking the chance. This whole week was a chance.

(-----fill in here getting into the room, drinks, sitting on couch, looking at view, more description of Eliot)

Monica watched him lean nearer as if she were observing from a distant tower. Shoes off, her feet tucked beneath her on the couch, she waited for his touch. The open collar of his pale blue shirt invited her to touch the spot where chest hair curled upward, a mixture of black and gray. The rolled cuffs bared strong forearms and hands. When his right hand flipped back the flounce of her skirt, revealing the top of her hose fastened to her black garter belt, distance evaporated. Lingering on the bare skin above the stocking, his fingers sent currents upward to warm and moisten parts of her too long neglected. She reclined a tiny bit, but otherwise waited, immobile. Her breathing gave the only clue to her eagerness.

Deftly, using both hands, he opened the top two buttons of her blouse, then lifted her hair and nuzzled the pulse at her neck. She tried to will her heartbeat to slow toward normal so he wouldn't know how erratically it responded to his warm lips. Her heart did as it chose. She followed, unbuttoning his shirt to the waist.

She gave a satisfied smile and said aloud, "That's coming along very well." At quitting time, eleven p.m., she stood and stretched her arms high, then bent forward to place her palms on the floor. After a minute's worth of deep breathing, she took off her wig, removed her makeup, brushed her teeth, changed into her white cotton gown, and crawled in bed.

Before breakfast the next morning, Jean was at Johnnie Lyn again. "Look, it's Wednesday and I can tell you're already getting worried about this—what to tell Audra, and depending, what to tell your mother, et cetera," she said. "I'm throwing in my two cents worth right now. You should do the speech. I don't think you need to volunteer any information to your mother. If you must tell something, tell her about the books. She'll get over it, especially if you point out the connection to the check you deposit for her each month. You don't have to mention me. Trust me, she'll get over it."

Johnnie Lyn knew if she ignored Jean, she'd be able to get through the day more calmly. But first, she said, "I doubt it. She's always lived by the rule that there's no excuse for lying. It's a sin. Plus, she's not that mercenary. "

"Tell her the publisher uses Gia's name to keep anyone from knowing it's you. No one in Archer City will ever know."

Johnnie Lyn said, "She'd tell me God knows."

She spent the rest of the morning on a chore she'd intended to complete for months. Since the beginning of Jean's career as an author, she had purchased numerous items she justified as research materials. Johnnie Lyn had said, "Buy what you need, but don't try passing those sex toys and other erotic stimulation devices off as business supplies. The IRS won't believe it."

At first, they'd been stored in the bedside table. A couple of years later, they were moved to a drawer in the chest. Then Jean had bought a trunk and promised she'd restrict her things to that space. So far, the still-empty trunk had not moved from the garage where it landed on the day she bought it.

Johnnie Lyn dragged it into the bedroom. She placed in it the contents of the drawer, frowning as she worked. Among the numerous research materials now assigned to the trunk were a dildo, vibrators in two different sizes, a package of bright red French Tickler condoms, unscented lubricant guaranteed to warm and stimulate, three bottles of flavored lubricant (no guarantee), star-shaped pasties with long tassels, and an empty whipped cream can. Then, in case she was killed in an accident and someone came to clear her belongings, she double-taped a label, PROPERTY OF GIA CARAWAY, across the trunk's top.

Jean went to work early that day and never said another word.

Often, Johnnie Lyn dreamed about her characters and their lives. Those dreams often presented her with the best of plots and many times with dialogue. A pad and pencil on her night table made capturing those subconscious messages simple. Thursday morning, before waking completely, she reached for the pencil. Minutes later, the blank page stared back at her.

Leaning against her headboard, shoulders slumped, she told herself she could take the day off. Perhaps her answer would come to her while she made a German chocolate cake. Mother would like that for dessert. She and her friends, three women from church, could enjoy it with their morning coffee all week. Johnnie Lyn knew they visited every day after the others' husbands went to work.

The trip to the grocery store for coconut, eggs, and pecans gave her an excuse to loiter. She took it. When she finished gathering the few items she needed, she chose the longest of the five checkout lines. Reading headlines on the tabloid covers, inching toward the cashier, she heard, "Johnnie Lyn, is that you?"

After a second's hesitation, she turned toward the woman behind her. "Yes?" That was a familiar face. She had no clue about the name.

The woman rescued her by filling the silence. "It's Charlene. You remember, from the English Department. How are you? Still teaching freshmen?"

By the time Charlene took a breath, Johnnie Lyn remembered her, the only other one who taught composition at the community college when she had. They'd often complained to one another in the faculty lounge. "No, I freelance, tutor, and substitute in the public schools to pay the rent." That lie almost told itself. "What about you?"

"I'm what people glorify by calling a full-time parent. Three children."

"Are you still writing poetry?"

Charlene shook her head. "Never got even one poem published, so I gave it up in favor of reading." She pointed to three paperbacks in her basket. "Romances, the trashier the better. You were writing serious fiction back then. Still at it?"

"Nothing serious." No lie in that.

Later, mixing the cake batter, the oven preheating, she arrived at a decision. When Jean turned up, she'd let her know she intended to follow her mother's advice, just quit procrastinating. Then she'd write Audra and say no to the conference and get the whole thing off her mind.

Three pans of chocolate batter in the oven, timer set, Johnnie listened to Jean while waiting for her computer to wake. Louder than seemed necessary, Jean said, "You waited this long, so don't decide until tomorrow after you hear what your mother has to tell you.

"What if she's found out about my name change or about the books, or both?" Just thinking about that nauseated Johnnie Lyn.

"If she has, she has, and telling Audra no today won't change that."

Johnnie Lyn nodded. She couldn't dispute the sense of that.

The computer's pleasant greeting chimed. She opened Jean's email program. Nothing there from Audra. Good. Then she checked Gia's fan mail. Nothing from Audra there either. She left the computer and stepped outside to move the garbage can from the curb to the garage. Two changes of clothes later, still not happy with the skirt and long-sleeved blouse she chose, she headed toward Archer City. The twenty-six miles took nearly forty-five minutes, even though there was little traffic.

Brightly colored pottery on Southwest patterned placemats decorated her mother's kitchen table. Johnnie Lyn placed the cake carrier on the cabinet. "Pretty dishes. Are they new?"

Her mother said, "Sort of. I've only used them once." She lifted the lid of the cake carrier. "We may need to eat dessert first. You made my favorite."

The cake had turned out perfectly, the layers smooth and a uniform height. Ordinarily, Johnnie Lyn had to skimp on the frosting because she invariably ate some, no, actually a lot, before she covered the layers. Today, the nausea had lingered. She said, "It smells like you made mine, too. Green chile chicken enchiladas. I should have worn a looser skirt."

Instead of her usual reply, encouraging her daughter to eat, fussing about her being thin, her mother said, "I found a low-fat version. So we don't have to feel bad about dessert."

Johnnie Lyn surveyed the kitchen, a child returning, watching for change. Taking care of an aging parent required vigilance. Her mother didn't require close monitoring yet, and Johnnie Lyn would acknowledge she wasn't very vigilant, but practice was important. She asked, "Have you been dieting?"

"Only trying to reduce fats and sweets. Well, except for special occasions." She pointed at the cake. "That's a special occasion." She opened the oven and bent to peer in. "Won't be long before the enchiladas are ready. I've also started walking thirty minutes a day at least five days a week. I don't want to develop diabetes like some I know."

They ate salad and enchiladas and agreed to let that settle before having dessert. But they stayed at the kitchen table where most of their real conversations had always taken place. Johnnie Lyn took a long time drinking iced tea, wiping the wet spot it made off the table. Her mother cleared her throat, then said, "I have something to tell you. I've worried about it all week."

Her mother's slightly flushed face looked more excited than worried. Then Johnnie Lyn noticed her mother's nails were painted a delicate shade of pink. And a slender silver chain bracelet with one heart-shaped charm hanging near the clasp circled her left wrist. How had she not noticed? Something had changed. That flush might be makeup. Johnnie Lyn sat forward, leaning toward her. She said, "Then tell me. I don't want you to have to worry. Maybe I can help."

"I'll start with the hardest part first."

Silence followed. Johnnie Lyn gave what she intended as an encouraging nod.

"I'm going to Montana for three weeks."

"That's great! A vacation. What about that worries you? Do you need money?"

"No, it's not that. It's all paid. I worry that you rely on me to be here. We've never been apart, not really, ever." She came to a halt again, took a drink of tea, sighed.

Johnnie Lyn made sure she wore a smile as she said, "Well, that would be accurate if you don't count the twenty-five years since I left for college."

"Yes, but you've always been near and we're in touch every day. I hate for you to be alone."

"I don't mind. And you said three weeks. That's not long, not really. Is this a tour group you'll be with?"

Holding up a hand, her mother said, "I started wrong. I need to tell you all of it."

Johnnie Lyn's mother examined the tea glass near her plate, touching its rim, then finally raised her eyes and began. "There was a boy I knew in Crowell, back before I knew your father. We never dated. Remember I told you a long time ago, I never actually dated anyone. But we talked sometimes at lunch. He was quiet and very smart and didn't play sports like most of the others. I'd wondered whatever happened to him."

Her right hand strayed to the tea glass again. Johnnie Lyn waited, hoping her silence made telling the story easier. When her mother started talking again, all her hesitation disappeared. For the next twenty minutes she explained they'd reconnected soon after she joined Facebook. He'd looked for her many times since he retired as a colonel from the Air Force years ago, had never married, and had returned to school and become a teacher. Now he taught in a small town in Montana, where he'd been for the past several years. After a few weeks of email that became a daily thing, they began Skypeing—her mother knew about Skype! This had gone on since January. In early May, he had traveled to Texas, but she didn't feel comfortable with his coming to Archer City.

"My friends wouldn't understand," she said. "We met over in Oklahoma, across the Red River from Burkburnett. Remember when I called you one evening to say good night and you said it sounded like I was in a noisy restaurant? I changed the subject. I was in the lobby of a casino."

Her mother stood, opened the silverware drawer, and handed Johnnie Lyn a souvenir spoon from the Kiowa casino travel center. "Alton, that's his name, said he never thought badly of me for getting pregnant. He understood why I had to leave town. One time, when he was in the Air Force, he tried to find that preacher's son. He wanted get a chance to punch him in the face and then to make sure he'd taken responsibility and supported us. I told him he'd paid some, but that I worked, and when you got old enough you did, too. I didn't want to sound pitiful, but still, it's true."

Johnnie Lyn never interrupted. Then her mother said, "So when he asked me last week if I would come to Montana, I gave it plenty of thought and a couple of days later I said yes."

She felt her mother watching her. Johnnie Lyn said, "Thank you for telling me. You shouldn't have worried about what I'd think. I want you to be happy."

Her mother sat silent, now holding the tea glass with both hands. Johnnie Lyn said, "I mean that. I want you to be happy."

"I believe you. For some reason, I feel like a different person, all of a sudden. Ever since I saw Alton. I'm not sure who I really am."

"Anybody you want to be, but you'll always be my mother." She picked up both their glasses, along with the napkin her mother had wadded into a ball. "Now can we have dessert?"

Along with cake, they continued talking. Actually, Johnnie continued listening and occasionally asking a question. Subjects her mother covered ranged from her now questioning the need to keep her hair long and dress plainly, she had decided there was nothing wrong with wearing tasteful jewelry, she planned to do all she could to stay fit, she wondered what she would tell her friends in Archer City about her pending vacation—she wouldn't lie—maybe just not tell everything, and lots about how good she felt in the presence of her long-ago male friend. Neither Johnnie nor her mother brought up the topic of where it all might lead.

Before she left Archer City, she'd gotten her mother to give her Alton's full name and address. She intended to run a search on him. For a second, she'd been tempted to offer her a set of Gia's romances, for instructional purposes.

As soon as Johnnie Lyn pulled away from the house where she'd grown up, Jean said, "You had the perfect chance to come clean, tell it all. Tonight you could have confessed you're a contract assassin, and she'd have said it was fine with her."

"I didn't want to spoil things for her."

"That's lame. You don't want her to know."

"Some secrets need to be kept for a while. Others longer. Mine should stay between us for now."

They rode the rest of the way in silence. Around ten, Johnnie Lyn drove into her own garage. She hoped to sleep and then wake with an answer for Audra. Instead, she spent the rest of the night sitting at her kitchen table. She thought about the last thing Jean had said. Not the part about being an assassin, but the idea beneath it—tell her mother the truth and do it now.

Jean didn't turn up again, so Johnnie was left alone to debate with herself. In the end, she knew that changing her name and writing erotica were not criminal, but the name change and the lies, if not the writing, were likely to hurt her mother. She'd think Johnnie Lyn was ashamed of her. For a few minutes, she even convinced herself keeping her mother in the dark was an act of kindness, sparing her feelings.

Even though Jean apparently had left, Johnnie Lyn could imagine what she'd have said to that—"so much crap." And then she'd have followed with, "Kids lie to their parents. Adults should know better."

Before dawn, without waiting to consult Jean, she wrote to Audra. The meat of the message was *I will co-present at the conference as you requested, on one condition. That is that I am introduced for the presentation as Gia with no mention of that name's being a pseudonym. Further, Gia will retire after the publication of this current manuscript. In her place, as Jean Barlow, I will launch a new series aimed at the 40-60 year-old female market. My research indicates their needs and desires are under-represented in current erotic romances. See the attached proposal for the series. I will await your reply before adding the conference to my schedule.*

Another cup of coffee waited in the kitchen. As soon as eight o'clock arrived, she called her mother. With enough caffeine, she could pretend she was brave. As soon as her mother answered, Johnnie Lyn said, "I enjoyed supper last night. And I wanted to tell you again how happy I am that you're happy."

A sort of giggle came from her mother, then she said, "Thank you, sweetie. I was afraid you'd think I'm an awful person. Or worse, a hypocrite."

"Never." Johnnie Lyn paused and took another sip of coffee. "I've been thinking about that cake. I'd love another piece, maybe two."

"I should have sent some with you."

"Is it okay if I come out around 10:30, coffee break time? We could have cake. There are some other things I'd like to talk to you about."

Her mother's voice sounded young, fresh, unburdened as she said, "I'd love that. You can help me choose what to pack."

When she clicked off the call, Johnnie Lyn returned to the computer. Audra's answer had arrived. *Dear Jean, my star of stars, It's a deal! New contract to follow.*

Johnnie Lyn raised her cup in a silent toast. Minutes later, she dressed in a pair of Jean's shorts and a sleeveless t-shirt. She added makeup and two bracelets. Then she checked websites for a full service salon and called for an appointment later in the week—for a haircut and color.

A Scent of Rosewater

Sitting at the desk, James looked up and to the left, a sideways glance at the mirror above the dresser. Not that he wanted to check his reflection; it wouldn't have changed—the dark, lean face his granny called pretty, the dreamy looking onyx eyes. He hoped to catch a look at the one he thought he'd seen watching him last night and the night before. Actually, he'd felt, more than seen her. He knew all about being watched.

Nothing there. No one. Maybe he'd imagined her. When he was a child, his teachers always commented on his lively imagination. His mother agreed, called him a liar. By the time he was eight, he knew no one wanted to hear about the people only he could see, the voices he heard. All they wanted—even his grandmother who loved him best of all her seven grandchildren—was for him to make them proud.

James stood and turned off the overhead light. The room didn't seem quite as cell-like in the light of the desk lamp. It wasn't really like a cell. This room at the Austin State Hospital Nursing Student Dormitory contained a comfortable bed, a dresser with a mirror, a desk, and a chair. More than he ever had at home. But he felt closed in, nonetheless. He raised the roller shade and glanced out the first floor window. He surveyed the hedge and the roof of the house behind, then focused on the wrought iron bars covering the window To repel invaders? So far, only a pair of pigeons that had managed to nest in the unoccupied room next door had breached the barriers. And the giant hissing cockroaches. Until the last two nights.

Seven p.m., and darkness covered the gray that lurked all day in the damp sky. He could go to bed, study, or listen to the radio. The correct choice would be to study—either for class tomorrow or the trigonometry he'd assigned himself to review. Pacing the short distance from door to window would accomplish nothing. He sat down again at the desk and turned back to the last page that looked familiar, trying to put his attention where it belonged. Psychiatric nursing.

He reread the first paragraph, about hallucinations. Easy stuff, nothing nearly as difficult as the organic chemistry he breezed through at college. All the instructors here at Austin State Hospital wanted them to do was memorize the categories of mental diseases, recite the symptoms, and learn not to be too afraid of or too understanding of the patients. The tests never included questions requiring any depth of comprehension.

First thing each class day, Dr. Anthony Lafitte, Attending Psychiatrist, paced the front of the classroom, chain-smoking and lecturing, never pausing to permit questions. After his cough-punctuated soliloquies, the doctor left, looking perplexed, as if he might have forgotten to emphasize some vital fact.

James hoped for the day when Lafitte would hurry back into the classroom and shout, "We don't really know why people go crazy. Just try to treat them with kindness. They are doomed."

He slammed the book shut. Last year during medical nursing class, James diagnosed himself with stomach cancer. Excruciating pain, change in bowel movements from brown to tarry black, weight loss. All within the space of two weeks. The symptoms fit, exactly.

The doctor at the student clinic at Wichita General told him that each year he saw at least three students with symptoms of life-threatening illness of one type or another. He said that in each case, the symptoms matched a description in the textbook they were currently studying. "You're surely not the first. Our minds do funny things to us," he'd said. James doubted the man, thought him patronizing. But as soon as he quit his extra job and took Maalox every four hours instead of Pepto-Bismol the stomach pain disappeared.

He reasoned that since this current class focused on mental illnesses, he'd probably start having paranoid delusions anytime now. He might exhibit waxy catatonia—the textbook showed a skeletally thin woman who looked like a statue—or maybe he would quietly slide into profound depression. *Lord knows I'm halfway there already.*

Scanning further, he searched for any hint about theories explaining depression. *If a person has reasons to be sick and tired of everything, is it depression or a realistic view of life?* Anger turned in upon the self, the explanation read. *Maybe so. But why does that qualify as illness?*

He returned to the page on hallucinations. The woman he saw in the mirror could be a psychotic symptom, or maybe merely an invention of his lively imagination. Or, one of those angels his grandmother always talked about.

James didn't need to study; he usually made the best grade in every class. "Get some sleep," he heard a voice say distinctly. That voice was no hallucination. It had lived with him since he was a child, telling him what was good for him, how to stay out of trouble, how to be best and first. It sounded like his grandmother. Tonight it went on to sing "How Great Thou Art." He lay on his bed, floating on the melody, and drifting near sleep.

He felt, rather than saw, a flicker of pale light from near the door. Without moving, he opened one eye. A woman stood inside the doorway, wearing an ankle length, high-collared, long-sleeved dress, holding a candle in her left hand. *Worse than I thought.* Not only a woman, he saw a blonde, blue-eyed white woman.

He closed his eye and sang softly along with his grandmother's voice. "Then sings my soul, my Savior God to thee. How great thou art." Only his lips moved.

A young black man swinging from a noose beneath a heavy oak branch, backlit by torchlight, had turned last night's dream into a nightmare. "Lusting after a white woman. Speaking to her in the street." Slurred shouts of white men emphasized the final twitch of the hanged man's limbs.

His entire body felt like a fist held tight for too long. James took a deep breath and wished for stomach cancer. With one quick move, he rolled out of bed and stood. No visitor in the room. He smiled a brief, tight-lipped smile as he recalled Granny's daily morning greeting. "New day. Thank you, Jesus." He would have welcomed her voice this morning, but he seldom ever heard it before evening.

He gathered his underwear, socks, and uniform and hurried toward the shower. Even though a second door opened on the opposite side of the bathroom, he had the facility all to himself. His own for the first time in his life. The adjoining bedroom and all four other two-room, one-bath suites in this wing of the dormitory were vacant. He wouldn't allow himself to dwell on the reasons for his room assignment—just take it—private bathroom, private wing. He hurried through his routine, avoiding looking in the small mirror until it was necessary in order to shave.

James left his room at exactly six forty-five a.m. The long hall from his room was populated only by shadows. The moldy smell that always lingered in his room gave way to the odor of pine oil the janitor used in the mop water. The single ceiling light cast weak fingers toward the dayroom. He passed the room's silent, blank television set, the two game tables, and the maze of empty plastic armchairs, and stepped out the front door.

As he had each day since he arrived, he paused a second before he passed the historical marker outside the dormitory. "Erected 1908 by the Austin Daughters of the Confederacy as the Home for Confederate Widows." His home away from home for the twelve weeks of the psychiatric nursing affiliation.

Anita Payne, a girl from his school, out early waiting by the bus, called to him as he passed the group she stood with. "Morning, James. Why don't you ride the bus with us? It's warmer."

He looked up briefly, showed her the careful smile he reserved for people who knew his name, and said, "I need the exercise. See you in class." Rosa Parks would probably have chastised him.

If there was anything to be thankful for here, it was the January weather. Wichita Falls would be windy and below freezing. To him, Austin's damp air felt near tropical.

The intersection at Guadalupe and 38th carried the only major traffic on the eight block walk to the Doctors' Dining Hall. He'd taken two steps into the street when a voice startled him into retreating to the curb. "Pay attention, James Raymond. Only people who keep their eyes on their goals succeed." This voice sounded like the preacher he'd tolerated every Sunday until he finished high school.

James muttered, "Thank you, preacher." Several cars sped past going north, disturbing the air enough to make him realize the voice had caught him daydreaming. More than once in that little church in Electra, the preacher stopped in the middle of his sonorous sermon and called from the pulpit, "James Raymond Lincoln, the devil sees you daydreaming. I pray he don't get you."

He didn't stop daydreaming in church, but he'd spent every minute in high school studying so he could graduate at sixteen and get away from all-day-Sunday church and that preacher.

The daydream that nearly got him killed in that intersection featured his high school in Electra, the one that integrated, for financial reasons, in the early fifties. He and the five others entered the previously all-white high school without any overt incidents. His daydream featured him as he took his place at the back of the classroom, homemade lunch in a paper bag on his lap, saying nothing unless a teacher called his name.

By the start of the school year in September, 1957, he lacked only four credits for graduation. Had he stayed until the following May, he would have been valedictorian. His family would have attended graduation, all eight sitting together, Granny stirring the air with her funeral home paper fan. His mother would have strutted in wearing a too-tight dress; his brothers fussing with their clothes, the six-year-old picking his nose. James chose to finish in December. Someone else could be first.

Next came work and college in Dallas, then more work at General Hospital in Wichita Falls. Now, nursing school. His daydream showed him trudging, head down, aimed toward medical school in the distance. Seemed like he'd never get to rest. He walked everywhere.

He looked both ways, and then sprinted across the intersection. Safe on the outer edge of the State Hospital property, he stopped, then breathed deeply to return his full attention to the present.

The memory of the woman he saw last night, or thought he saw, returned briefly, but did not linger. Hunger urged him toward morning reality and the Dining Hall. The aroma of freshly baked cinnamon rolls welcomed him at the door. He took two, added milk and an apple, and thanked the baker behind the counter who looked puzzled and mumbled, "Sure."

Patients from the Alcoholic Ward did most of the work in the Dining Hall. The two assigned to clear tables, barely able to do the job, looked like they had spent years with bottles to their lips. James ate quickly at a table near the back of the nearly-empty room, scanning his notes from Dr. Lafitte's lectures, raising his head only when a patient came to clear the table. The rotting-fruit smell of paraldehyde rode on each of the man's shallow breaths. James couldn't avoid the odor of the chemical meant to cushion withdrawal and prevent DTs.

Although nursing students were never assigned to Ward 8, Alcoholics, he'd learned more than he wanted to know about delirium tremens as an orderly on the Colored Ward at Wichita General. He left the dining room; the apple remained on the table.

In class that afternoon, Dr. Lafitte's ceaseless striding from one side of the classroom to the other almost hypnotized James. He stayed awake, but didn't attend to the lecture. Theories about schizophrenia, nothing more than rationalization as far as he was concerned, floated from Lafitte along with clouds of Lucky Strike smoke, one as beneficial as the other. Blame schizophrenia on the family dynamics, blame it on genetics; might as well blame it on voodoo.

Pretending to take notes, he wrote a list of his goals. Instructors appreciated students taking notes. James usually liked seeing his goals spread before him. Number one was "finish psychiatric nursing. The fifth, final, one was "Attend Howard University Medical School." The preacher's voice intruded, "Stay focused." James knew that obnoxious voice spoke truth. He placed his right index finger on the words "psychiatric nursing."

After Lafitte left and the class returned from a break, they found the desks arranged in a circle. The instructors said eye to eye contact encouraged group interaction. Students from each affiliating school tended to cluster together: Dallas Methodist; Ft. Worth General; Hallmark Baptist, Tyler; Jefferson Davis, Houston. His school, Wichita General, was apparently the only one that took note of Brown v Board of Education and admitted a black student, a male, at that. In Wichita Falls, the school's dormitory housed only females, so he only saw the other students in class or on the wards. That was fine; group interaction held no interest for him.

Discussion began with a follow-up on Lafitte's lecture. The instructor described a hypothetical patient who saw non-existent people and heard voices. She asked the likely diagnosis and proper nursing action. One student said, "Paranoid schizophrenic," then rattled off something about reorienting the patient to reality. Another one said, "It doesn't matter what the diagnosis is, a person who hallucinates is mentally ill."

James controlled his tone and said, "If I understand the textbook correctly, not all schizophrenics are paranoid and not all hallucinations are due to schizophrenia." He didn't elaborate; didn't ask the question he wanted answered—what distinguishes hallucinations from imagination? All that was necessary for the class discussion grade was to contribute. He saw the instructor mark on her tally sheet. No one else in the class said a word.

Next, the instructor lectured about social support. She described research demonstrating that people with strong social support were less likely to suffer mental illness. Then she gave instructions for an exercise. "Put a dot in the center of a blank sheet of paper. List your family and friends in concentric circles around that dot at distances that represent how close you feel to each person."

James created an elaborate series of ever-expanding circles of names around the spiky star-like dot he used to represent himself. The teacher didn't ask them to turn in their sheets. James frowned. He had invented some interesting names. He wadded his "social support" and jammed it into his uniform's pocket.

Sunday, two college trigonometry books, paper, pencils, and peanut butter cookie crumbs competed for space on his desktop. The A he had received in trig at college reflected only that he did better than his classmates; he needed a much deeper understanding of the subject to pass the Medical College Admission Test. So far, he hadn't opened a book. He stared at the paper decorated with the star and fictitious friends.

"Social support be damned," he said. He smoothed the wrinkles from the paper then took his time folding it, half, then continuing until it fit a space two inches square in the palm of his hand. With each fold, he stated one question after another about the validity of the research the instructor mentioned. Debating, because although he wasn't convinced friends were necessary, neither was he sure social isolation was healthy. Logical conclusions require supporting evidence. His only evidence was that he'd done fine so far without friends.

The preacher, who seemed to have displaced Granny, had been at him all morning. "You should spend your time in church on the Lord's Day." James opened a trig book, stared at a diagram that made no sense. Then he shut the book and waited. The woman he saw in the mirror would come; she did almost every time the preacher berated him. Never saying a word, she only smiled, which he took as encouragement. This time he would look at her, not just her reflection. *Why not? She's my only friend.*

He never had seen her actually arrive. He didn't know if she opened the door and walked in, passed through the wall, or simply materialized. He knew she wasn't an ordinary human. Or maybe she was. He hadn't tried to touch her, certainly wouldn't.

From what he saw in the mirror, she wore no makeup and no jewelry and looked about thirty—not young or old. Each time, she wore the same dress, that old-fashioned, long-sleeved one that seemed to be made of cotton printed with tiny roses.

Maybe he'd imagined it, but he thought last night, when she came with her candle, he'd smelled roses, too. Maybe glycerin and rosewater like his grandmother used for her hands. Remembering the scent and his granny, he had cried, big tears, silently. Cried for the first time in a very long time, and in front of a woman he didn't even know. She told him not to be embarrassed. Not that he actually heard her voice. Not like he heard Granny, or that preacher, but he heard the thought. Clear as could be. "Don't be embarrassed, my friend; cry if you feel like it."

The trigonometry books waited. Let them. None of it made sense today. He hadn't slept a full night in the four weeks he'd been here. Some of the time, the voices kept him awake. Other times the dreams kept him tossing. Not that he'd ever seen a lynching, but the stories the older people at home told had etched the images in his mind. His imagination did the rest.

A long walk might help, but he didn't know the neighborhood, wouldn't risk being arrested. Life would be different when he finished his education. He lay on his bed and closed his eyes, hoping for a visit, thinking of rosewater hand lotion.

Monday morning, he overslept—from Sunday afternoon, all night without waking. The hot water pipes' vibrating jarred him awake. When morning demand taxed the showers, hot water arrived as a gift; unexpected and surprising, accompanied by clattering pipes. He hurried past the dayroom and waved briefly in return to a greeting from one of the girls in his class, then looked away. Even if he'd wanted to, it wouldn't be safe to make a friend of her.

He skipped breakfast and went directly to the Houston Unit, a separate building north of the Dining Hall. For the rest of their Austin rotation, eight weeks, the students would be on their assigned units all day Monday through Thursday and until noon on Friday, with the only class on Friday afternoon. Apparently they had learned all Dr. Lafitte could teach them. From now on, it would be the nurse instructors only. Fine with him. At least they didn't smoke in class.

The nurse instructors would only talk about the nurse's role. He could bullshit his way through any test they put in front of him. The nursing they talked about had nothing to do with reality on the units. They described a mental health facility where nurses talked long and thoughtfully with patients, and administered treatments ordered by doctors. Here, the only registered nurses on the units were the head nurses who managed the schedule and did a few things the Psychiatric Techs weren't allowed to do. Otherwise, techs ran the place.

As soon as he stepped into the Houston Unit, he understood why he was the only student assigned there. Apparently everyone in Houston who was mentally ill was black. Naming the unit Houston must be code. Back in Wichita Falls they still called things what they were—Male Colored Ward at the General, Colored Waiting Room at the bus station, White Only water fountains in every public building.

The Charge Tech who greeted him, Robert Mason, occupied most of the nurse's station. His broad frame, muscular arms and legs, and wise eyes created a presence in the tiny space. The man had probably been in charge all his life. His voice, a smooth bass that belonged in a choir, betrayed kindness. James felt himself lean forward. He managed a smile.

"People from Houston get to come here as soon as they're admitted, instead of going to the receiving units. Men on this side, women in the back part of the building." He raised an eyebrow just a fraction and his smile edged toward a smirk. He pointed to another tech out in the dayroom with the patients. "Harold Jackson, day shift."

James tried to ignore the odor that surrounded them— urine, cigarette smoke, sweat—like an ancient pool hall somewhere on the wrong side of the tracks. He did his best to control his breathing and look interested. Patients who weren't staring at the television set mounted high on the wall or mumbling and staring at the floor studied him as he passed. James stayed close to Mr. Mason.

"Your instructor sent a copy of the course outline and a note saying to let you get oriented for a couple of days before assigning you a patient. Pretty much left it up to me, other than that. I doubt we'll see her over here," Mason said.

"Whatever you think will help me learn. Just tell me what to do," James said. He could tell from the way the other tech watched Mason, if anyone there had something to teach him, it would be this man.

Class preparation for Friday required a verbatim report of an interaction with a patient and an analysis of the student's thoughts and feelings about the conversation. Apparently Mason had read the course outline. Thursday, he told James he should choose one or two patients to spend time with so he could do the assignment.

James chose one of the cleaner-looking men he'd seen often playing dominoes with other patients. Mr. Mason agreed. "He's was here about this time last year, got a little better when spring came. Went back to Houston. He was once a medic in the military. Sad, what happens."

James waited until a patient sitting near Mr. Thomas shuffled toward the bathroom. He sat in the newly vacated chair and said, "Good afternoon, I'm James Lincoln, a nursing student. Want to play dominoes?"

The patient, looking toward an empty chair on his right, said, "He one of us? What you mean?" He turned to face James. "They say you is one of us."

Mr. Thomas squinted, leaned close. James edged back in his chair. He said, "I'm a student nurse. Name's James. Want to play dominoes?

"You one of us. They told me."

"Who told you? I can't see anyone here with us." James uttered that sentence just as he'd read it in the textbook. Reorient the patient to reality, the book counseled. He felt foolish as he said it. *What reality?*

"They not here, but they talk to me."

"Often?" James felt his throat tighten; he could hardly speak above a whisper.

"Most every day." The patient straightened in his chair and looked directly at James for the first time. "That's how I got here. I sleep on the street most the time. Come January, cold weather, I start telling what they say to me, mumbling, acting scared. In the bar and in front of the grocery store. Pretty soon someone comes out to get me, bring me here. They think I'm crazy. Not too. It's warm here. Plenty to eat. Only thing to watch out for's old Sparky. "

James kept his expression neutral. "Old Sparky?" Another textbook response, reflecting the patient's words.

"Uh huh." Mr. Thomas nodded toward a patient sitting, drooling, in the next chair, wearing urine-stained pants. "Sparky got that one there." He pointed to the dominoes. "You shuffle. I go first. You keep score. Pay me in cigarettes."

He drew seven dominoes and concentrated on setting them upright. A smile changed his face, gave him a crafty look. He turned over the double five. "Write that down. Ten points."

James stared at his dominoes, shook his head. No fives. He drew another one from the bone pile, then a second, before he could play. He felt the patient's eyes on him as he placed the five-one. Mr. Thomas whispered, "Yessir. You got that look. You one of us. Watch out, boy." Then he looked right and left. "No score. My turn."

Now, in his room, near midnight, James still had not written his report for class. The blank sheet of paper on his desk might as well have been stone and he without a chisel. If he inscribed the patient's words on paper, they would be real, permanent. Hearing them had been bad enough; having a teacher read them would be worse. He wouldn't do it.

He didn't. Instead, he concocted a three-sentence summary of a long, silent game played with a fictitious patient who couldn't match the spots on the dominoes. His analysis explained that he had felt he had benefited the patient by creating a caring climate.

If Mr. Thomas knew, who else could tell? "Keep this up and they'll get rid of you for sure. That's exactly what they want." The preacher. *Where had granny gone?* He knew the answer—where she'd been all along—in that tiny cemetery in Electra in a grave no one bothered to tend, covered by sand in the winter and goat-heads in the summer. The preacher was the only one who talked to him anymore.

In the three weeks following his domino game with Mr. Thomas, James had managed to keep busy when he was on the unit, walking the dayroom's edges with patients who paced, helping some make cigarettes from bulk Bugler on the roll-your-own machine, playing whist, and avoiding Mr. Thomas. Mr. Mason asked him a couple of times if he was okay. James said he was fine and thanked the Charge Tech for asking. He didn't speak in class and wasn't called on.

All that prevented the preacher from keeping him up all night, every night, was the lady with the candle. When he turned his light out and got in bed, she came and sat in the chair at his desk, smiling encouragingly. Even with her there, his trig book remained closed. Sleep was the only thing he seemed able to accomplish.

Last night, she didn't come. He was left alone with the preacher, listening to his accusing tone as he ranted and finished up with a flourish—"You must mend your ways now, focus on your goals, be ever vigilant. Stop listening to that white woman you think is your friend. She wants you to sleep your way to failure. Follow me. Do only as I say." It sounded like the altar call at church. James heard the choir singing "Sinner Come Home."

This morning, his hands shook as he dressed. Walking to the hospital, he felt as if he were wading in heavy sand. The phrase "softly and tenderly Jesus is calling," repeated endlessly in his head. The choir's soprano sang off-key. He knew from the gnawing sensation in his stomach and the way he could breathe only in short, shallow gulps, that something was bound to happen today.

When he got to the Houston Unit, James set to helping Mr. Mason count out the morning Thorazine doses. He'd seen in the patients all of the drug's negative side effects mentioned in the textbook—shuffling gait, uncontrollable tongue movements, and slowed speech. But in his weeks on the unit, he also had seen some patients' behavior change from extreme, violent agitation to almost docile calmness. Maybe some patients weren't doomed, but only destined to shuffle and speak slowly. He willed himself to focus on counting pills into plastic cups.

"Today you'll learn something you won't forget," the tech said. "Assist with electro-shock treatments and help recover the patients afterward."

James dropped the Thorazine bottle. He stopped breathing. The Houston Unit psychiatrist favored EST as the treatment for both severe paranoid schizophrenia and profound depression. He closed his eyes and forced himself to inhale. He'd heard the techs say this doctor enjoyed doing the treatments— gave twenty to every patient rather than the usual ten. His method regressed some patients until they were unable to recall their names and had to be fed. James knew now why dread had surrounded him like a coffin this morning.

The first patient made no sound as the doctor inserted a protective tongue guard into his mouth. James gently restrained the man's arms when he flailed during the seizure, and held his own breath as he waited for the patient's respiration to return to normal. He pushed the gurney to the recovery area where a tech watched for signs of aspiration until patients returned to consciousness.

When James returned to the treatment area, he watched from the doorway as two techs guided the next patient to the table. James' legs belonged to someone else; how he made it to Mr. Thomas' side, he didn't know. His domino partner looked up at him and mumbled, "Never tell no one what you hear."

The doctor frowned and inserted the tongue guard. He turned the dial on the shock machine, raising the voltage. "This patient is a chronic schizo. He's been here three years in a row, more severe each time. This is the last hope for eliminating his persistent hallucinations."

James wondered whom the doctor was trying to convince.

The seizure mimicked grand mal epilepsy's uncontrolled tonic and clonic muscle contractions. Mr. Thomas' mucous membranes turned dusky blue as his breathing halted and did not resume for a full minute. James' legs and arms felt uncoordinated, as if he also suffered the seizure. The gurney supported the weight of two as he transported Mr. Thomas to the recovery area.

The rest of the morning's treatment session seemed to last for days. Instead of following when the patients returned the day room, James went into the restroom, slammed and locked the door, then fell to his knees in front of the commode. He vomited, bile bitter against his tongue. Violent spasms continued long after his stomach emptied.

When he gathered the strength to stand, he washed his face and rinsed his mouth. Then he walked slowly to the nurses' station. He said, "I have to go to the dorm. I think I have the flu."

Mr. Mason, his bass voice making one word a pronouncement, said, "Go." No one else spoke a word.

Walking to 201 West 38th Street took him thirty minutes instead of the usual twelve. Each step required concentration; each intersection challenged his coordination. He knew what he must do. He only had to get to the dorm to do it.

The janitor nodded as James rushed past the dayroom and down the hall toward his room. The door resisted and nearly defeated him. He closed his eyes and saw himself huddled, twitching in seizure spasm, on the floor next to that flimsy, ancient piece of wood and its rusty lock. *Where is the preacher when I need him? Or Granny?*

"Your problems will soon be solved. Be calm, take your time." He heard his own voice saying the words aloud. After a deep breath, James turned the handle. The door opened smoothly. He paced the small distance from door to window, and stared through the bars. There was no hurry, now that he knew what he must do. Just wait for his strength to return.

He lay on the bed and stared up at the beam crossing the ceiling and supporting the single light fixture. The bulb became the only thing in the room, aside from his thoughts, as he waited.

It seemed soon, but must have been hours. Sleep had fallen on him like a shroud and dark had replaced dim gray daylight before he woke. Without moving, he returned his eyes to the bulb, expanded his gaze to the beam. He imagined the too familiar scene, one he had visualized so many times before— when fatigue from working long hours and outrage at the poor care patients in the Colored Ward received overwhelmed him— when he could barely contain the urge to scream at his brothers to stop wasting their lives drinking and to take responsibility for their children—when the immensity of the years of hard work ahead of him made him hopeless.

Intense concentration kept him from hearing anything other than his heartbeat. Before, rage and weariness fueled his despair and drove him to exhaustion before the end of the scene. Today, fear tinged the vision that progressed steadily, demonstrating his only answer, the final tableau that showed him beneath a tree or beam swaying like a slow pendulum until he stopped, out of time. Fear that Mr. Thomas was right. "You one of us, boy."

He felt the weight of someone watching. She sat at the desk, he knew, but he wouldn't meet her gaze. He stood, removed the bedspread, and stripped off both sheets, the first procedure a nurse learns. But this bed change was not to comfort a patient. He tore each sheet into two long pieces which he tied together and braided. Next, he knotted the two braids together end to end to make one long, strong piece of fabric. No rush, take your time.

Then in a sudden spasm, he stood in the middle of his mattress and reached for the beam; it waited, but just beyond his grasp. He flung the homemade rope against the wall. It lay on the linoleum, useless, impotent as the rage that knotted his stomach.

He crossed the room and pulled at the heavy desk. Something held it, resisted his effort. He wiped sweat from his forehead. The woman in the old-fashioned dress held tightly to the opposite side of the unyielding piece of furniture. "You can't stop me," he said. "I may be like them. But I won't tolerate it."

She didn't answer, but released her hold.

James pulled again and the desk slid easily. He shoved the bed toward the window and positioned the desk under the beam. Picking up the braided sheets, aware for the first time of their weight, he dragged the chair next to the desk, scraping it loudly against the floor. He stopped, lifted the chair, and placed it down quietly. He glanced toward the door, shook his head. *Who would have heard? The janitor and I are the only ones who set foot back here.* He stood erect, as if he'd found a small store of new strength, and raised his right foot toward the chair.

From behind him, a touch, the size of a small hand, pressed against his shoulder. The substance and warmth of an embrace folded around him. He felt the safety he remembered finding only in the expanse of his granny's lap. The touch moved him irresistibly toward the bed, to a rosewater scented haven on the bare mattress. The lady visitor patted his back the way a mother soothes a baby. *I don't have to do this.* He recognized the voice, his own, and no one else's. And he cried, sobbed until there were no more tears. He felt her there, protecting him. And he knew she was part of him, part of what made him different. Then he slept, feeling her arms around him and knowing peace he hadn't felt since Granny died.

The next morning, James woke hungry. He looked toward the empty chair and tried to imagine his lady visitor sitting there again. All he saw were the braided sheets; he heard nothing except the radiators' rattling.

As he left the dorm, he passed the students' bus waiting at the curb. He continued slowly to the end of the block. There he stopped and then reversed direction. When he reached the bus, he got on.

Nowhere Near

Carl left after he ate his breakfast, gone to check the cattle and whatever else he occupied himself with each day. Veta knew he'd be in at noon; he was not a man to miss a meal. She had managed to get her main chores done early. The chickens were fed; eggs gathered; and house made passable since she seldom had company, at least not any wearing white gloves. Both hands in dishwater, the radio still giving the morning news—same stories the second time around since it was just after seven—she thought she'd take a few minutes for herself, do nothing at all, except maybe drink a cup of reheated coffee.

Staring through the window above the dishpan, Veta had to shake her head at her foolishness years back, making those fancy curtains to hang there, calling attention to it. What she should have done was board it up and paint over it the color of the walls. The only thing to see out that window was the bathroom door four feet away. Why she was concerned about that today, when the view had been the same since Carl plumbed in that bathroom twenty years ago, she had no idea. It wasn't likely she'd get him interested now in taking out the window and walling up that space.

They weren't the only people on this stretch of country road with odd rooms cobbled on over the years. Still she cocked her head and said, "Well." Those escaping thoughts happened now and then since Ma died and the girls were gone. No harm in keeping herself company.

Her widowed sister-in-law's house a mile north hadn't been plumbed until five years later. Of course, the other one, south a mile, had made sure she had all the conveniences in place before she agreed to marry. Veta secretly called that one Carl's brother's wife.

She'd washed that final plate twice and started in a third time when a horn sounded, first out front, then closer, probably out the back door near the cellar. She rinsed the plate, jammed it in the drainer, and swiped her hands dry on her apron. So much for time to herself.

Before she could get to the back door, Veta heard Carl yelling but couldn't understand his words because he never let up honking. With the hand he didn't need for the horn, he waved her over to the pickup. "Get in. Now! You've got to see what they done. Killed 'em both....Tore out the fence... Burned ..." He kept talking, but none of it made sense.

From looking at his eyes, Veta could tell he was scared, not joking. She ran to the house and rushed back wearing her jacket. The November wind pierced, even in full sunlight. She barely had the old pickup's door shut when he accelerated, making a wide turn that scattered the hens, sent them squawking toward the chicken house. Only the rooster stood fast, flapping his wings and stretching his neck as they sped past. At least driving kept both of Carl's hands on the steering wheel so he couldn't hit the horn again. Trying to sound calm, she said, "Tell me what's wrong."

"You'll see. You won't believe it, but you'll see. Get my twenty-two from under the seat. Pull out that box of bullets in the glove box. And that knife."

Veta did the best she could not to slide across the bench seat as he turned onto the county road going south and then swerved west onto the turnrow next to the wheat field. She flipped the glove compartment open and pulled out the box of twenty-two caliber long rifle bullets and the skinning knife. Leaning down to fish under the seat, she lurched when he bumped over a cattle guard. Her head hit the dashboard. She slammed the knife and the box of bullets on the seat beside him and said, "Slow down, if you want me to get that gun. I can't do it if my neck's broken."

He didn't answer, but the veering stopped, and then just as she got hold of the rifle, he slowed to a crawl. Veta rearranged herself upright on the seat, and braced against the dash with her right arm, the gun now lying across her lap. It might be loaded for all she knew.

Then he stopped, grabbed the twenty-two, and said, "Get out slow, don't say nothing till I give you a signal."

Following him, not saying a word, skirting around the occasional cowpie, she sneezed, stopped still and sneezed again. Something in the air, something burnt smelling.

Without turning around, he said in a raspy whisper, "I told you to be quiet. They may still be here." Then he squatted his bulky frame down, as if that would hide him on that wide, flat, grass-covered piece of West Texas. Nothing made sense this morning. But she did the same thing, knowing that getting up would be a chore. Her knees weren't what they once were.

Hunkered down in the foot-high brown grass, Veta looked toward the south, the nearest fence line. As if peering through binoculars suddenly focused on a distant object, she startled, felt herself edge slightly away from the now-clear view. A stretch of the fence, at least two hundred feet of it, lay on the ground, strung out into the field as if some playful child had plucked it up, trailed it along, then tired of it and left it behind. Cedar posts that had been set in concrete, now broken off level at the ground and still anchored in the barbed wire, measured the fence segments like frets on a giant's guitar.

Looking farther to her right, toward the center of the pasture, she searched for cattle. This three hundred twenty acre field of bluestem was where Carl grazed the pregnant cows along with their previous year's calves. They were the first of the herd he'd begun building—sixty total now, after starting with thirty. New calves would be born in the spring.

Getting into cows and calves was branching out, he'd said, after all the years farming only. He'd said it was a good move financially, using up more words than he usually spent talking about his motives. She'd nodded, knowing it was more likely keeping up with his younger brother, Conrad, who preferred raising animals to doing the hard work of farming. Or maybe he needed something to take care of, now that the girls were both married. Whatever his reasons, when he called for her help when the calves were born, she saw in his eyes what looked to her like interest, for the first time in a long time. Then his favorite cow dropped the first bull calf and interest gave way to happiness, something she'd thought he forgot how to feel.

She spotted them. There, far in the northwest corner, a clutch of reddish-brown bodies with white faces huddled and milled. She couldn't squat any longer. Catching hold of the back of Carl's belt, she hauled herself up to stand. He pulled a bandana from his coat pocket and wiped at his face, then said, "Don't move. See out there, that burned patch? And those two cows, laid out dead? That's why the rest bunched up over in that corner. They're afraid."

The two dead cattle lay in the middle of a blackened circle, maybe sixty or seventy feet wide, hard to tell that far away. She said, "How could that burn and not set the whole pasture afire?"

"They can do things we don't understand." He drew in a deep breath, never taking his eyes off the dead cows, or maybe he saw something she didn't. He said, "You go call the sheriff, and I'll stay here, just in case."

She wanted to ask in case of what, but didn't, just put her hands in the pockets of her jacket and hunched her arms close to her chest to stop the shaking. As she started toward the pickup, he said, "Call Felix, too. He needs to see this."

"I will, then I'll come right back. Do you want me to get Bud?"

"No. He's useless as teats on a boar. Call Baby Sister. She'll wonder about the sheriff being out here. Tell her not to mention it to Bud, nor anyone else."

Driving to the house, the heater turned on high, Veta made her own plan. Thought about Carl calling Sharasue Baby Sister again. Even after their daughter told them Bud said a married woman shouldn't be called baby anything, Carl would forget.

Getting Felix out here made sense. Carl trusted her uncle more than he did anyone. Older by twenty years, Felix had been around, had worked in the oilfield, and now made his living buying and selling cattle. But instead of turning at the driveway to their house to make calls like Carl said, she drove on north the quarter mile to Sharasue's place. Veta had an idea she might need her.

In less than ten minutes, she'd called the sheriff and Felix, and she and Sharasue were in the pickup, on the way back to the mystery in the pasture. For once, Veta was glad Bud was such a no-count who stayed gone most of the time. No explanation required. Not as long as Sharasue got back and had a meal on the table and a smile on her face when he came in. Whenever that was.

No time now to think about useless husbands and mistreated daughters. The sheriff would be there as soon as he could make the twenty-five miles from Wichita Falls. She pressed the accelerator, knowing the dust rising behind them would announce her return. A matching dust plume showed in the distance in front of them—either the law or Felix or both. Whichever, she thought Carl would feel better having men around to talk to, to puzzle out who had done what had been done, and why.

As if they had planned it, she and Felix came to a halt in the field she'd started thinking of as the devil's pasture within about one minute of each other. She and Sharasue hung back a little while Carl showed Felix the damage. He pointed out the ruined fence, the huddled Herefords in the far corner, the two dead cows, and the perfect circular line burned in the grass around them. Veta heard him say, "Looks like a bull's eye in a target, don't it?"

Carl waved her over. "Go take a look at those two cows. You won't believe it. Looks like a butcher worked on 'em. Hollowed out real neat."

One look was all she needed. No wonder Carl had gotten into high gear. Someone, or something, had been there and slaughtered those animals and burned out a perfect circle around them. No one who'd seen her wring a chicken's neck and cut the bird up to fry ever accused her of having a weak stomach. But something about the sight of those cows brought her close to vomiting. She backed away a few steps, then turned and went to stand by Sharasue, away from that awful sight.

The sheriff and one deputy pulled up in a big black SUV just after Felix had pronounced his judgment on the whole thing. All he'd said that Veta could hear was, "Damn strange." Then he and Carl stood together, talking, while the sheriff's vehicle took its time getting to them from the county road.

The lawmen drove out nearer the dead cows, then got out and walked around the carcasses. The deputy took some Polaroid pictures, hunkering down to get close up shots. Veta moved closer and Sharasue followed. Before long, the sheriff and his deputy concluded that vandals had chosen their farm at random. Speaking directly to Carl, as if he was the only one there, the sheriff said the troublemakers had been slick enough not to leave a single track coming or going, and that they might be part of a gang traveling across the United States, maybe involved in some sort of devil worship. According to him, 1975 had been a big year for cattle deaths in other states in the west. The deputy added they'd read a lot of reports from Utah just in the past month, for instance.

Carl didn't say a word, just raised an eyebrow and pulled a toothpick out of his overall pocket, stuck it in his mouth. Felix asked about aliens, space creatures, to which the sheriff made a face somewhere between a sneer and a smile of the sort that people aim at the less fortunate. He gave no answer at all.

The men wearing badges seemed untroubled by the perfect circle of burnt grass and what seemed to Veta like surgical precision used to remove the reproductive organs and tongues from the animals. The deputy drawled, "Coyotes," as if that explained it all.

Felix said, "Coyotes with acetylene torches?"

And then, like he hadn't heard, the sheriff said, "Keep us informed if you have any more trouble."

After the two drove away, as she and Sharasue walked away toward the pickup, Veta heard Felix tell Carl, "I hope he don't think I'll forget that come next election. There's more to this than a gang of vandals. He's too damn lazy to bother investigating."

Sharasue hadn't said a word the whole time. Looking at her sitting straight as a poker in the pickup seat, hands in her lap, Veta wondered when she first started shrinking, making herself fit into smaller and smaller spaces. She asked, "What do you think?"

Sharasue kept staring through the windshield as she answered. "I was wondering why, if aliens did come, why they'd kill innocent cows, not get rid of someone who needs getting rid of." Then she turned toward her mother with a smile full of teeth, startling in contrast to the dark hollows below her eyes. "I watched too much Twilight Zone when I was little, I guess."

Because she didn't have anything sensible to add about the dead cattle or the sheriff either, Veta yelled out the window at Carl, "I'll go back to the house and make coffee."

Sharasue said she had to be home, Bud might be back soon. So Veta stopped long enough to let her out at her house. She hadn't said so, but she remembered Sharasue watching Twilight Zone, and never taking it seriously. She'd been more interested in buying lipstick and going to the skating rink to flirt with boys.

When Carl finally came in, late that afternoon while she was making cornbread to go with supper, she said, "I worried about you when you didn't come in for dinner."

"Had some things to do. Don't you worry. I'll take care of you. Everything is going to be fine. Just remember to do what I say."

Then he turned silent, busying himself getting out his shotgun, going through the process of breaking it down and cleaning it. Until then she hadn't noticed his hands shaking. He didn't sleep that night; she knew because she didn't either.

Early the next morning, the editor of the local weekly newspaper turned up at their front door asking questions. Carl told him he'd been misinformed. No story on Wilson Road. As the man drove away, Carl said to Veta, "Never did like him, even back when we were kids."

The truth was, Carl didn't like most people—not that he disliked them, he just didn't spend any effort on liking. Even back when he courted her, 1939, he'd seemed different from what she expected. Although her only source of information about what to expect from boys or men was from watching her dad and her brother, both easy-going men cowed by her mother's spells. That and what she overheard from girls who sat together way in the back on the school bus. But sitting up front, as she did, made it hard to gather much from the snatches she heard between their silly giggles.

Mrs. Wilson, Carl's Ma, had been a regular at the Church of Christ as long as Veta could recall. At the age of sixteen, her mind hadn't been cluttered with too many memories, so she was pretty certain that neither Mrs. Wilson's husband nor either of her boys ever came to church. Then that year, after Mr. Wilson's funeral, Carl started turning up at services with his mother on Sunday, both morning and evening. Veta also remembered she didn't pay him much attention; he was old. But when he began finding reasons to talk to her, she didn't mind, even if he never joked and his conversation had mostly to do with farming and the weather. After all, he was a grown man, twenty-one at the time. And when he invited her to dinner after church one Sunday, she saw that no one else at his family's table traded much conversation either.

She picked up her coat, preparing to gather eggs, and said to Carl, "What do you intend to tell people? Someone will ask me at the grocery store or church, I'm sure."

He sat down at the kitchen table where he'd been before the knock at the door. From behind the sports section of the day-old Wichita Falls paper, he said, "It's nobody's business. I intend to take care of it. Don't you worry."

Out at the chicken houses, she worked quickly, shooing the hens off, gathering eggs until her first basket was full. Then she slowed, not eager to go back in the house. Even though this was her day to deliver fifteen dozen to the grocery store like she did every Tuesday, she needed to get her thoughts straight before she drove the twelve miles to town. Whatever was the answer to who killed the cattle and all the rest, she had to agree it was no one else's business.

She tried to come up with other possibilities to solve the mystery while she transferred chicken feed from the bags it came in to the tight-lidded bin where she stored it, telling herself as she did it she wasn't wasting time. She ran out of busywork about the same time she came to the conclusion she might never know what or who killed the cattle. So she tended to the business of getting the eggs ready to go to town. Carl would do his best to take care of her. He always had. The word steadfast came to her mind, somehow making her feel calmer.

In the kitchen, Veta heard him from where he sat on the porch. "Turn out the lights. It's time to go to bed."

His voice interrupted her watching a trail of pissants cross the cabinet top. Scattering them with a swipe of her dishcloth, she marveled at how quickly they reformed their line, each ant bound to do his duty. She wasn't surprised at Carl's words. Why would tonight be any different from any other since November when the cattle were killed?

No matter what the clock showed, he gave that order as soon as it was dark out. From nightfall on he sat out there in that metal chair with his shotgun on his lap, a toothpick in his mouth. She knew his routine. Every thirty minutes, he pulled the watch from his overalls pocket, looked at it and nodded, replaced it in the pocket, then stood and walked all the way around the house, stopping on each side and peering through his binoculars off across the fields in all directions. Then he'd situate himself on the front porch again. He'd come in to bed at different times. She guessed he was being cagy, not sticking to a predictable routine in case anyone was watching. And guessing was what she had to do—he didn't explain himself and wouldn't even if she asked. After thirty-six years married, he probably thought she read his mind.

In December and January, when dark came just after six, she'd spent a lot of those nights staring at the ceiling, thinking, remembering things she thought she'd forgotten. Focusing on their first daughter's wedding made her smile into the dark. Carlene had never been a minute's trouble. She finished high school in three years and had a college degree three years later. Then that day when she married, it was to a good man a few years older. If a person asked for a perfect family, Carlene's would be the model. Veta would've been happy in the dark, if all she recalled were the good times. She wished she'd lost memory of the year of her own wedding. That was the year of her mother's worst spell, the one that ended with her at the state hospital. Everyone had agreed there was nothing else to do with a woman who ran naked into the yard, chasing her husband with a butcher knife.

Another complete recollection, including the iodine smell of the hospital delivery room, and the bad-penny odor of placenta blood, was Carl's disappointed face when their first, Carlene, was born. He probably didn't intend it to show. And the same scene, different baby, when Sharasue came along two years later. Worst of all those memories that visited in the dark was the vivid purple and blue of the fist marks on Sharasue's face one night not long after she married. Veta could still hear her crying to Carl, "No, Daddy, Bud didn't mean to hurt me. He promised it won't ever happen again."

Veta didn't seem to have control of what visited her at night. In the light of day, she could manage to focus on work to be done, or force herself to think of happier times—there had been quite a few. But those nights had worn on her. Then two weeks ago, with the arrival of March, the residue of glumness piled up behind all the sad memories must have shown. She knew for certain that the constant vigilance had worn Carl. His face bore a permanent scowl, and walking or sitting, his head down and shoulders slumped, he looked like a huge dog restrained too long on too short a chain.

Taking care not to make it sound like a challenge, she said, "I'd like to read a while before bed."

"You'll have to do it in the dark. No lights."

When she didn't answer, he yelled inside, "You heard me."

If someone had been listening to that and didn't know any different, they'd probably laugh. Surely he meant it as a joke. She knew better. That first time he demanded she turn out the lights was just a few days after those dead cows, four months ago. He and Felix had spent a lot of time pacing around the burnt field and rebuilding the fence. By the time the posts were all replaced and the wire restrung, Carl was convinced a spaceship had landed out there. He'd told her that a return visit was likely before long.

Standing at the kitchen sink thinking about how small things could change without her noticing, she stared at the cast iron skillet in her right hand, the familiar object suddenly foreign. She thought she'd gotten it clean.

Little differences that naturally occurred over time seemed normal, not really like changes. Her chickens laid eggs, then nested, then had chicks cheeping around behind just the way life was supposed to run, she always assumed. Carl planted wheat, then if the rain came, wheat grew. Seasons changed, but never abruptly. Days passed, so little different each from the next that she wouldn't notice how one day she'd have to put on a sweater when she gathered eggs, then a few days later, it was a coat. She just reached into a different spot in the closet.

Plunging the skillet back in the suds, she scrubbed away the flecks of fried chicken coating, then rinsed and dried the pan. The porch rocker's metal base scraped on the concrete, sending a shiver up her neck. As if the sound had been a siren, she turned out the kitchen light, then the bedroom lamp. A little extra sleep wouldn't hurt her.

He came to bed in the dark; she didn't know the time. The bed sagged toward his side, the one nearest the door. He grunted and his right work boot—always the right first—thudded to the floor, the left, seconds after. The bed shifted, relieved of his 250 pounds as he stood again. Overalls and shirt slapped against the floor. Without opening her eyes, she could see them draped like a dirty shroud over the boots and socks. The bed covers flapped and the sour odor of sweaty feet followed the full weight of him, owning the air in the room and his side of the bed.

She sat up, then stood, facing away from him, toward the curtain-covered window. He said, "Where you going?"

"Bathroom."

Navigating in the dark on her way out of the kitchen, through the hall, she passed the empty bedroom where she'd spent so many hours caring for Ma. At the time his daddy died, Carl, his older brother's widow, and Conrad each got a third of the land. Carl, unmarried and living with his parents at the time his daddy died, had been the one to get the home place. With the house came responsibility for his Ma. As it worked out, once they were married, Carl had the house and land, and within a year Veta acquired the responsibility of tending to the poor soul suddenly invalided by crippling arthritis. That woman lingered six years almost immobile and racked by pain, occupying that room until the day she died, with never a bedsore to suggest any neglect. Looking back, Veta realized it was good she'd been seventeen when they married. She'd had plenty of energy then.

Without turning on a light, Veta rinsed her hands and started toward the bedroom. Just then she heard Carl shout, "Veta, get down on the floor! You okay? "

The beam from his flashlight shot across the floor toward her where she'd hunched. Any other time, seeing him in his baggy underwear and holey T-shirt would have made her smile. Carl's bare feet slapped against the ancient linoleum and then he reached to help her up. He said, "I heard a shot, maybe two."

She hadn't. Maybe lack of sleep made him hear things. She asked, "Which direction?"

He pointed toward Sharasue's house, then jerked on his overalls without a shirt and shoved his bare feet into his work boots. Without another word, he beckoned for Veta to follow him to the porch. On the way, he picked up his shotgun and put down the flashlight. All the lights were on at their daughter's house. But not a sound came from that direction. She said, "I could call."

"It's three in the morning." He caught hold of her hand. She didn't know what to make of that. Then he said, "I'll stay out here and watch."

"I'll stay with you for a while."

They sat side by side in the metal chairs, silent for a long time. He rose and made one of his circuits around the house. When he returned, he said, "I never told you, didn't want you to worry, but I changed my mind. Last week. I don't think it was aliens from space killed those cattle. If it had been space creatures, they'd have already been back."

"Who then?"

Just then she heard a man's voice shouting. Carl pointed with the shotgun barrel toward their daughter's place. When the wind was right, sounds traveled the distance across that wheat field between their houses clearly as if it they were separated by a few feet, not a quarter mile. Seconds later, shouting again, Bud slammed out of the front door, continued yelling toward the house, and then threw something toward the front door. A crash of breaking glass told Veta he'd thrown a bottle. Most likely a beer bottle. She looked at Carl, whose attention focused on their son-in-law, now revving the engine of his pickup, leaning out the window, yelling at the top of his voice. All she heard clearly was, "You bitch, I'll teach you to argue with me."

They watched as he sped out onto the county road and headed toward town. Then the lights in Sharasue's house went out, one by one. Neither of them spoke for a few seconds. Then Carl said, "Sitting out here I seen that little bastard coming in and leaving at all hours, heard loud talking, cussin', always him, not Sharasue. Then it came to me. I wouldn't put it past him to have gotten some of that no-good bunch he runs with to help him kill those cattle. He wants to scare me, get me out of the way somehow, so I can't watch over our little Baby Sister."

Which was worse, his thinking it had been men from Mars or Sharasue's husband? Neither idea gave Veta much comfort. She said, "I'm glad you told me." She couldn't help yawning. "I'll find a way to talk to her, see if she has any reason to fear him. I mean any new reason."

"You go on to bed. I'll keep watching."

She slept so soundly the rest of the night, she had no idea when he came to bed, or if he did. Over fried eggs and coffee the next morning, Carl told her that Conrad might be in the scheme with their son-in-law. "He's already told me, and who knows how many others, he thinks I've gone crazy. Felix heard him spreading that at the coffee shop last week."

"Who'd believe him?"

He shrugged and said, "Maybe lots. People love to believe the worst, if it makes a good story."

Gossip did tend to spread, and never in a positive direction. She'd witnessed that when her mother had her bad spell. Church people had been the worst, as far as she could tell.

As soon as Carl left, she walked to Sharasue's house and knocked on the door. This being a Saturday, she wouldn't be at work. An hour later, all Veta could say for sure was that their daughter had lost weight in the week since she'd seen her last and "Everything's fine, real good." As she walked back home along the county road to where her chickens waited to be fed, Veta repeated aloud what Sharasue had said when she'd asked her straight out if she and Bud were having trouble. "It's a wife's duty to help her husband. You taught me that." She still couldn't figure out how that answered the question.

Midmorning, Conrad's wife showed up at the front door. She said, "I was just thinking we hadn't visited in forever. So I said to myself, I'll just take care of that this very day."

It wouldn't do to be inhospitable to Carl's brother's wife, so Veta invited her in and offered her coffee and some cookies. She was tempted to ask if her visitor had come for any particular piece of information, but didn't. After several minutes of listening to talk about the weather and nodding about the divorce of some daytime television show's main character, Veta learned the reason for the house call.

Leeora said, "Conrad and I have been concerned about Carl. Is he doing better?"

"He's doing fine, real good. What makes you ask?"

"We know he's having trouble with reality, thinking there are spacemen coming on his land, killing cattle, all that. It had to worry you. And someone said they heard he expects them to come back, that he's waiting for them every night."

"As you know, people will say anything to see what kind of reaction they can get from gullible folks."

Apparently not finished with what she'd come for, Leeora said, "Now I know you've probably already looked into this, but I have the name of a good doctor I've seen. There's medicine these days for problems like this. It's not like it was back when your mother got sick."

Before she answered, Veta drew a long deep breath, and considered counting way past ten. "Since you only moved here from Archer City in fifty-three, I doubt you have any accurate information about my family at all. So I'll thank you not to speak of my mother. And no, I have not looked into medicine or any doctors. There's no need. Carl is nowhere near crazy, which is what you're implying. He's saner than most of the people walking the streets around here."

She stood and held out her hand for Leeora's cup. "I'm sorry to rush you, but I have chores to do. Thank you for stopping by and thank you for your concern." She waited until the woman rose, and followed her to the door. Veta said, "Oh, I meant to ask, how's Conrad? Someone at church mentioned they heard he'd been ailing."

"What? No, he's not sick."

"Well, like I said, you can hear anything."

It took Veta several cookies and a large glass of milk to get herself settled down after that. She decided not to tell Carl about the visit, at least not yet. It might do more harm than good. That evening, she did report to him on Sharasue, but didn't mention her seeming thinner. Carl said, "About what I'd expect. Saying she's bein' a good wife. Well, we'll see." Soon after that it was time to put out the lights.

She remembered the sound he made settling into the porch chair and then later, his getting into bed. Finally, she relaxed and let herself sleep deeply. Sometime later, she tried to tell herself she was dreaming, the way sleepers will do, and tried to make herself move even though she couldn't. In that dream, a large hand covered her mouth, threatening to smother her. Panic made her eyes open, and she realized there really was a large hand there, smothering her. Each movement she made, squirming, trying to get away, caused the hand to push harder.

Then the hand moved from her mouth and she sucked in a breath. Fear kept her from screaming. Before she could move from the bed, something rigid and cold pressed against her chest. Even though she couldn't see on that dark night, she smelled gun oil and knew it was a shotgun barrel. A voice she didn't recognize at first said, "I knew you were one of them. All this time, you've been sending them information."

"Carl, Carl!" she screamed. "Carl, it's me, Veta! Put that gun down. You're scaring me!"

She heard a gasp, as if someone surfaced after too long underwater. Then Carl's normal voice said, "Veta?"

Her heartbeat, booming in her ears, made speaking a chore. Carl ended up sitting on the bed, as if his legs had given out, or his will to stand. The shotgun clattered to the floor. After the trembling in her legs stopped, she went to the kitchen for a glass of water. When she came back, she found him still sitting on the bed, his head in his hands, leaning forward with his elbows on his legs, worn down by constant vigilance.

She sat beside him and put a hand on his back. After a long silence, he said, "I think I was dreaming, sleepwalking. You looked like a stranger, maybe part of a gang. I'm so sorry."

She wondered who, what gang. But he was so shaky, she didn't ask. She said, "You need to get some rest. All this watching has worn you out."

"Please don't tell anyone."

"Don't scare me like that again."

Carl slept the rest of the night and most of the next day. He got up after noon and ate biscuits and bacon and went back to bed again. The morning after that, he asked for coffee and took a shower.

He announced he was going to change things up, not stay out on the porch every night, but do it on different nights, skip some. "That'll mix them up. Sooner or later, they'll be back."

She didn't ask who.

April first, a night with no moon out, he yelled from the porch for her to turn off the lights, as usual. She did and then went on to bed. Accustomed now to being awake in the dark, she seldom actually went to sleep until midnight, after he came in the first time. Then on those nights he was on guard, he'd get up later and go back out to his post. He'd stay out through two or three of his inspection tours around the property and then come to bed, then a couple of hours later, he'd get up and repeat the cycle. She'd adapted to this new routine and had convinced herself he wouldn't try to kill her, now that he was getting more sleep.

That April night he didn't come in at midnight. She waited a while and then tiptoed across the room to peek out. He'd fallen asleep in his porch chair, his head bent forward, swaying a tiny bit with each breath. The shotgun and binoculars lay beside the chair. She hoped he hadn't swallowed his toothpick.

Habit sent her to the bathroom, walking like a ghost or a sleepwalker through the rooms. Then, instead of going directly back to bed, she passed noiselessly through the kitchen and out the back door. She intended to admire the stars, take a look toward Sharasue's place, and then get back to sleep. It wouldn't hurt if she left Carl asleep in the chair.

All the lights were off at Sharasue's. Bud's pickup sat parked beside the house. All was quiet in that direction. The big dipper shone clearly. The star at its bottom—she didn't know its name—actually twinkled the way the nursery rhyme says. Calmed by the vastness, she walked slowly toward the door.

Flashes of light, low on the horizon off to the west, caught her eye. Her hand on the screen handle, she watched as the lights grew nearer and assumed the shape of a large blimp, or maybe a gigantic cigar. Never good at estimating distances, she had no idea how far from her the lights were, but gradually they came closer until she felt bathed in light. Surely that would wake Carl. For what seemed like a very long time, the lights hovered above the ground. Then as slowly as they had appeared, they rose and faded into the distance. She stood watching, holding back to keep from waving goodbye to it, wishing the light had lasted longer.

In the house again, as if she'd only made a small detour on her way from the bathroom, she peeked out on the porch. Carl slept on. She didn't wake him, telling herself it was her job to take care of him, to encourage him to rest, and not to worry him. As peaceful as everything seemed, she lay awake in the dark, wondering what she'd just seen, if she indeed had seen anything. And for a few minutes, just before falling asleep, she let herself wish that whatever she saw had come down had taken her away to someplace where people laughed.

The next day she didn't mention the lights. In the following few weeks, the new chicks hatched, the calves were born, and each day brought a few more minutes of sunlight.

Nineteen Fifty-Eight Was a Long Time Ago

Driving from Odessa, where he and Delta parked the trailer last night, Buddy told himself the two men he was supposed to meet in Crane wouldn't ask him many questions. Actually, most things they might ask wouldn't bother him, just the one he didn't want to answer out loud. He hated lying, but it would be more than he could tolerate telling strangers how little he knew about his own father and worse yet, trying to explain why he'd waited until he was sixty-four to come looking for answers. Surely they wouldn't ask.

Once he hit the north edge of Crane, he slowed to match the posted thirty miles per hour speed limit. After poking along two blocks farther, he made a small salute to the city policeman he saw backed onto a side street operating a radar gun. Heading south, he came close to running out of town. Then he saw a sign pointing off to the right—PLEASANT VIEW—with the words Assisted Living and Skilled Nursing Facilities in small letters below. They'd told him it would be easy to find, the only one in town.

On his left another large sign announced TEXAS DEPARTMENT OF CRIMINAL JUSTICE HOBART UNIT. The small letters on that one said Do Not Pick Up Hitchhikers in This Area. Buddy turned right.

As soon as he entered the front door at Pleasant View, an odor of urine mingled with something meant to disguise it, faintly cherry scented, made him cough. Buddy recognized the smell as the same one that nauseated him at the nursing home where he'd had to put his mother years ago. He stopped, took a long breath, and thought about going back outside. It wasn't as bad as the smell that had surrounded him all day long, every day, back when he drove a cattle truck. He'd get used to it in a few minutes. While he stood considering escape, a woman in a pink scrub suit startled him. Without rising from her seat behind the large circular counter in the center of the building, she said in a loud voice, "Can I help you find someone?"

Buddy got closer so he wouldn't have to shout his answer. "Yes, I came to see Elmer Goins and Bill Snider. They're expecting me. Name's Buddy Bell."

She pointed to the nearest hall on the right, one of four that led, like spokes, from where she sat at the center desk. "They're in room one ten." Same loud voice. It must come with the job. With that, she went back to whatever she was doing when he walked in, giving it her full attention.

"Thank you, ma'am." He started toward the hall, then returned to the desk. "If they're allowed to go out, I'd like to take them to lunch after while. Would that be okay?"

That made her take notice. She still didn't get up, but she closed her magazine and looked at him a long time before answering. "Are you family?"

"No, ma'am, just a friend." He didn't try to explain he'd never seen them before, but that he was pretty sure they'd be pleased to get out for a while.

"They're both able to go out if they want to, but we'll need your identification. You have to sign out and sign them back in."

"If they decide to go, we'll come by here and do all that before we leave. If that's okay."

She nodded once, saving her energy, he guessed, and returned to her magazine. As he crossed the lobby toward the hall she'd pointed him to, he noticed a large glass cage hanging on the wall holding live birds—several wrens and a single yellow canary. He wondered if those tiny birds were too old to fly.

Television news, volume loud, reached him as he passed room 108. He had half-expected to hear distress cries from behind the closed doors along the hall. But the broadcast coming from 108 was the first sound he'd heard. The rooms could be empty, or all the occupants might be asleep or unconscious or just waiting. The worst would be waiting—skeletal women and men in uncomfortable beds, eyes staring at nothing, lying on urine-absorbing pads, waiting for anything to interrupt the string of empty days. Being unconscious would be merciful. He'd do almost anything not to end up anyplace like this.

He knocked on the door to room 110. Quiet conversation in two different voices preceded a loud reply. "Come on in, whoever you are."

From the doorway, which was as far as his gumption carried him, Buddy said, "Hi. Sonny Bell was my father. I'm Buddy, the one who called. Are you Elmer and Bill?"

"What's left of 'em. I'm Bill. Come on in."

He didn't look like a man who belonged in a nursing home. Standing erect, he offered a hearty handshake. With his clean shave and creased Wranglers, he seemed ready for the coffee shop. Then as they shook hands, Buddy saw that Bill was looking past him and off to the left a little. The unblinking right eye was glass. The iris in the other was clouded milky white. Bill did a good job of pretending he could see until he waved his left hand toward the television set and said, "That's Elmer, my roommate." Elmer sat in a recliner on the side of the room opposite the television, wearing a sad smile and shaking his head as he watched Bill's effort to be hospitable.

Elmer said, "Buddy, you'll have to pardon me if I don't get up. Haven't got my leg strapped on yet." As punctuation, he lifted the short stump that had been his right leg. "Come on in and let's visit."

Buddy steered Bill toward the other recliner by gently touching his elbow. That left the visitor the choice of an uncomfortable-looking straight-backed chair or either of the twin beds. He perched on the chair. Since it seemed like they were waiting on him to get things started, he asked, "Y'all have family in town here?"

That was all the prompting it took. They spent a fair amount of time giving him the complete rundown. Pared down, it amounted to both without family, they had become roommates after their physical conditions made living at home alone difficult. Bill said, "I got in touch with Elmer just before he decided to move in here. We thought it might be tolerable if we was roommates. Some days, the only thing that is tolerable is my roommate. This place can sure wear out a person's good humor."

Elmer, the one he'd talked to on the phone, had gotten his leg on and now stood, taller than Buddy had expected. "We've both been thinking about your dad, since you called. Remembering."

Bill had Buddy located now. He faced him directly and said, "Yeah, I do remember old Sonny. We worked together in McCamey and then over at Iraan for sure, and I think maybe a couple of other places. He'd work a few months and then he'd quit and head back to where your mama and you kids lived. Where was that?"

"Levelland."

"Yeah, Levelland. I guess he worked some of those little fields up there, those times."

Buddy said, "Sometimes when he was home, he'd pick up some midnights. Other times he'd rest a while and then be gone again."

"That's the way it was with a lot of oil field guys. Specially if they had a family. I been tryin' to recall more about him. One thing I remembered right away is that he'd always be the one the tool pushers and the drillers would count on to teach the new guys what to do. See, Sonny was real smart and real patient. You ever do any oil field work?"

"No, sir. Drove tank trucks a while. Then later I got on doing long haul and kept at it. You know, the oil field always looked like awful hard work to me."

Elmer, pacing over by the window, looked like he was getting his leg limbered up. A tiny squeak marked each step, but otherwise, he moved okay or at least as well as any guy who'd spent a lot of years doing hard, dirty work did. Buddy had seen old cowboys with both legs who didn't get around as well.

Elmer said, "You're right about that. Hardest work I ever done was roughneckin', working midnights on them old rigs. Did that more years than I wanted to. Later on, I moved up to being a tool pusher and it got a little easier. Hardest part of that was bein' blamed for anything that went wrong."

Bill laughed. "Yeah, you got your share of blame. You remember that well over by Big Lake when we got to about four thousand feet and lost the bit down the hole? Couldn't fish it out for shit—took about six days. To hear that promoter tell it, the entire thing was your fault."

They traded stories for nearly an hour. The pain in his back and legs, his unwelcome companion for the past four months, competed for Buddy's attention. His tolerance for the straight-backed chair ran out at about thirty minutes into their recitation. Finally he said, "Say, what do y'all think about getting out of here?"

Elmer said, "Think about it every day—got no place to go."

"I was talking about lunch, maybe at that place I saw on the way over here—the Dairy Fluff."

"Sure," Bill said. "Ready when you are."

Elmer said, "Aw, I hate to miss—let's see, it's Friday, that means we'll miss meatloaf and peas and tapioca. I don't know. Maybe we ought to stay here."

Bill looked in Elmer's direction, then Buddy's, locating his audience, then he said, "Well, I hadn't thought about the tapioca. You may be right."

It took a minute before Buddy joined their laughter and asked, "You two practiced that, right?"

They were on their second cups of coffee since finishing lunch. All three had eaten chicken-fried steak from the buffet. Buddy had watched the two of them working as a team getting their food. Elmer described the choices as Bill slid along the one tray they shared. Bill softly named each item he wanted and his friend put it on his plate, then dished his own helpings. With no assistance at all, Bill grabbed an extra roll and stuffed it in his shirt pocket. Then, carrying the tray, Elmer walked slightly in front of Bill, who used his friend's elbow as a guide moving to the table.

After they all three sat, Elmer located each item on his roommate's plate, speaking so quietly Buddy could barely make it out. "Steak at twelve o'clock, French fries at two, pinto beans at six, sliced onion at nine, and a roll at eleven." Elmer winked at Buddy and said, "As you can see, we're a team. I get him where he needs to go and he holds onto me to keep me from tripping on my wooden leg."

Later, Elmer went back for seconds on the scalloped potatoes, but had passed entirely on the salad. He said he only liked iceberg lettuce, not that stuff that looked like spring weeds. As Buddy recalled, Sonny Bell never ate salad.

The conversation never lagged. They entertained him, and each other, with tales about wells blowing out, drillers who had been drunk on duty, and recollections of injuries sustained by men on the rigs.

Finally, because he couldn't hold back any longer, Buddy asked the main question on his mind. "Did either of you know anything about how my daddy died? All I ever heard was what Mama told us, that it was up in Wyoming about nineteen fifty-three. He'd have been about forty-one or two by then."

Elmer looked at Bill. Bill stared straight ahead. Neither answered for a while. Buddy stirred his coffee and watched a waitress scoop her tip off the table next to theirs.

Bill cleared his throat. "Maybe I'm thinking about a different old boy. I could be wrong, but I seem to recall working on a job with him back in nineteen fifty-eight up at Kamay. They were water-flooding some of those old leases that were playing out."

"Nineteen fifty-eight?"

"I could be wrong. Could've been someone else."

"No, I believe you're right," Elmer said. "I saw you and him both there, lots of times when I was working at Holliday. Remember, we all went over to Vernon that year to the rodeo."

Buddy exhaled loudly. After about a minute with no one making a sound, he said, "Doesn't that beat all? We'd heard Wyoming, nineteen fifty-three. I was seventeen at the time, still living at home."

Elmer said, "Maybe he went back to Wyoming; maybe you had the year wrong."

"Do you remember anything else about him being in Kamay?"

Bill cleared his throat again. "Maybe this is bringin' up bad news, but I remember some woman he was going out with there. Elmer, do you recall her name?"

Elmer nodded. "I sure do. Martha Clay. Seemed like a real nice woman, kinda good lookin' too. Worked at a bank in Wichita Falls, I'm pretty sure."

Buddy couldn't find a real word to use then, could only make a noise. It came out, "Humph."

Bill said, "Hope it doesn't make you feel bad to hear that."

After a long hesitation, Buddy realized his new friends had both stopping drinking coffee and started watching him. He said, "It might have back in fifty-eight, but not anymore. I'd like to find out whatever happened to him, though—you know, what he died of and where. Or maybe he's alive."

"Well, sure. Maybe we can help. There are a few more of us left from back then. We've got telephone numbers for five or six. If you want us to, we could call them."

"Yeah, making phone calls would beat making trash baskets out of egg cartons in activity period the next few days," Elmer said. "Course that would mean I'd miss spitting snuff juice in my coffee cup to upset old lady Branson. That's the only reason I even go to activity time."

"I'd be much obliged," Buddy said. "Yeah, that'd be real helpful."

He stopped at a convenience store on the north side of Crane. The glass door of the refrigerated case reflected a face that looked familiar, but older and sad. He made himself look past to the rows of cans and bottles. The names blurred. He opened the door and grabbed the nearest silver can. At the checkout counter, the clerk said, "Is that all? Just one beer?" It took him a bit to realize he'd handed her a Coors Light.

"Wrong can," he said, as he made his way back to the case.

She frowned and shook her head when he returned with a Diet Coke. He paid and left before he could do anything else stupid.

He turned off of Highway 385 onto the first gravel road he came to. His next turn put him on a pumper's road. A man shouldn't be behind the wheel if he can't keep his mind on driving. Right now, the only thought he had, the one he heard himself speaking, was, "Daddy, why didn't you take me with you?"

He parked the pickup and stared at a cluster of storage tanks and a single large pumpjack painted black and orange. Usually, the slow stroke of those large, powerful pistons pulling oil from a deep well seemed orderly and peaceful to him. Today, all it did was ask him if he really wanted to dredge up things that had been buried for so long.

It seemed as if he didn't have a choice, because when he leaned back in the seat and closed his eyes, he was fourteen years old. He walked into the kitchen, and his mother and both his sisters, sitting at the table, stopped talking. Mama's thin-lipped, sour smirk, Janine's glare, and Annette's eyes rolled toward the other two made him try to explain. "I came to get Daddy and his friend a beer."

Even then he couldn't tell who spoke first. But they all three, Mama included, rained such hateful words at him that he pretended to be deaf while getting the last two beers out of the refrigerator. "Let him get his own." "Who does he think he is turning up here once in three months?" "Acts like everything's all rosy." "Got us living in this tacky house on the wrong side of the tracks." "Bringing in that dirty roughneck with him."

Knowing he was fifty years past that day, he could still remember what he'd thought as he carried the beer to his father. "Please don't let Daddy hear them. He'll leave again and this time he'll never come back."

None of that made a difference now, he knew. Neither one of his sisters would care; Momma was long dead; and the fact of the matter was that finding out what his daddy died of, if he'd died, wouldn't get him a bit closer to knowing what might be causing his own pain and all the other symptoms he knew were slowly killing him. But right this minute, that day all those years ago was all that mattered.

Running away from dealing with whatever was ailing him had only made things worse by bringing up what he'd buried a long time ago. And he'd done a good job of complicating everything in the process. He knew the most direct, sensible thing to have done when his troubles started would have been to tell Delta, go to a doctor, and deal with whatever had to be done next.

Instead, he'd convinced himself Delta deserved a vacation and then, after it was over, he'd tell her something bad was wrong with him, and they'd both be in good shape for him to start letting some doctors do what all needed doing. Now that they were down here in the Permian Basin, and it was convenient, it only made sense to check out the two old roughnecks. He'd planned a little speech to justify the surprise vacation, so it would sound sensible to Delta. But he never had to use it. As soon as he suggested taking a trip, the only thing she asked was, "When are we leaving?"

Later on, when he told her about making a jaunt to see the two men who'd known his daddy a part of their vacation, she'd given him a long look. But even then, she didn't ask any questions. All she said was, "Anywhere away from home is fine with me."

Thinking about it now, he probably hadn't fooled her at all. It didn't matter. Today all his worries about the pain and fatigue and all the other ways he wasn't himself seemed smaller, pushed to the background. They'd been replaced by an emptiness that opened inside him when he found how wrong he'd been about his father, and when he then began to wonder what other lies he'd built his life on believing.

The Diet Coke hadn't cured the vacant feeling occupying his chest, but after he finished it, he left the lease and headed north again toward Odessa. Buddy drove slowly and by instinct, not really seeing the flat dry scene he passed through. If he was correct, those two old roughnecks back there in Crane were living out their days in a place that was a cross between a storage facility and a prison. And the image he'd constructed years ago, of his father resting in a grave in some public cemetery in a small, windy Wyoming town near an oil field, had been built on a lie. If Bill and Elmer were correct, his father was probably buried in some small, windy Texas town near an oil field. Or he could be in a place as sad as Pleasant View.

It was late afternoon by the time Buddy got back to Odessa. Situating the pickup across from the trailer took more effort than it should have. He finally got it right on the second try. He'd parked their trailer at the local hospital's RV lot, after telling Delta it was part of the vacation surprise. They'd stay at hospitals wherever the spaces were offered free, just for the fun of it, and also because most of the commercial RV parks in West Texas were next to railroad tracks.

Moving slowly, Buddy stopped to aim his keys at the pickup. The lights blinked once as the doors locked. He rolled his shoulders and tried standing up straight, but it didn't last. The only thing he could see was the pavement a couple of feet in front of him as he walked toward the trailer. He heard Delta's voice from behind the trailer's screen door. She said, "Hey, mister, are you lost or should I be suspicious?"

He looked up and gave her a smile, picking up his pace. "Lady, if this is Odessa, I'm not lost. What about you—what are you doing here in this parking lot with this trailer set up?"

"Planning to go into business." She winked at him. "I

just haven't decided what my business is going to be." She opened the door for him and reached out to hug him.

He held her close for a long time, kissed her for a long time, then said, "The only business you need to be concerned about, ma'am, is being here with me."

He sat in his recliner, managing to do it without groaning. Instead of picking up his USA Today, he stared out the screen door.

Delta said, "Something bothering you?"

"Puzzling more than bothering. Soon as I think about it a few more minutes, I'll try telling you."

Getting that out took all the strength he had. Delta must have been able to tell, because she said, "I was about to take a walk to that little park. We can talk after you have a chance to rest."

When she came back, he said, "Thanks. I needed to sort it out." He paused, then started in. "Two main things got me down today. First, that nursing home. The smell hit me when I walked in. I could have overlooked that, probably, but the entire situation gave me a bad feeling. It just seems so sad that these two old guys, both able to keep themselves clean and get around, have to live in that place, mainly because they don't have any family. They were happy to go out to eat, and they made good conversation. They help each other like brothers.

"But there they are in that place that's like a warehouse for sick old people. Those two'd be fine if there was some good place to live where someone cooked and checked on them once in a while; some place where there were things that old men like to do besides watch television."

He sat forward in his recliner. The footrest flopped down. "Delta, it scared me. I don't want to ever end up like that. And, I don't want those old roughnecks to have to stay there either. Okay, one of them's blind and the other one is missing a leg, but other than those things, they're able and—I'm not doing a good job of making this make sense, am I?"

"Did they mention anything that made you think they were being mistreated?"

"No, I doubt if they are. It's more like just being stored there till they die. I feel like something ought to be done, like I ought to do something."

He was quiet, pressing his temples and forehead with his fingertips. He stopped and sat up straight. He knew he could tell her. She wouldn't try to talk him out of how he felt. She'd listen and understand. He shifted and faced his wife. "And then there was the second thing. They told me that my daddy was alive and working in Kamay, Texas, in nineteen fifty-eight. That's five years after we heard he died in Wyoming. Who knows, he may still be alive—may be living in some place like that nursing home. I just don't know what to think. Maybe Mama knew and didn't tell us, or maybe she was already—you know how she got. I need to find out, though. Kamay is the only place I know to start, where they said they saw him last."

She nodded, staying silent. He stared at his hands, not meeting her eyes. He told her the rest of what they'd said— Martha Clay, all of it.

He said, "Hell, I don't know—nineteen fifty-eight was a long time ago. Maybe it doesn't make sense to even try to find out anything. What difference does it make? That's what my sisters would say. What do you think?"

"I think you're right, it was a long time ago. But you should do what will be best for you. Find out if you need to or let it be. It's up to you."

A week later, after he and Delta had seen all the sights Odessa and Midland had to offer, including the life-sized replica of the Globe Theater and the West Texas version of Stonehenge, he pointed the pickup south again. At the nursing home in Crane, Buddy passed by the desk ungreeted and apparently unnoticed by the woman at the desk, the hefty one he'd seen before. This time she was reading *Cosmo*. Elmer and Bill were ready, freshly shaven and dressed.

"Hey, Buddy," Bill said.

"How did you know it was me? I could have been that fat gal from down at the desk."

"Nope, she never moves. We were expecting you. And I recalled the sound of your boots."

Elmer said, "We skipped breakfast, hoping you'd want to go to the Dairy Fluff again."

"Well, I don't want y'all to starve. Let's go."

Elmer and Bill ordered eggs, bacon, biscuits, and gravy along with their coffee. It was all served family style, large portions in big bowls. Buddy had a small amount of scrambled egg.

"You're eatin' light, Buddy," Elmer said.

"I already ate once, before I left Odessa. Y'all are gonna make up for me, it looks like."

"This is the first gravy I've had in six months," Bill said. He lifted a forkful of gravy-covered biscuit to illustrate. "You know gravy causes cancer."

"I don't guess I'd heard about that," Buddy said. He wadded his paper napkin and then smoothed it out and refolded it.

Elmer and Bill both nodded. Elmer said, "It's a fact. See, they used to serve gravy over at the home. It was the only thing they had that made it seem anything like home. Then about six months ago it just disappeared. No more gravy. The only conclusion we could reach, and we discussed it quite a lot, was that it must cause cancer. They were doing it for our own good.

"Thing is, at our age, most of us would just as soon take our chances with cancer as give up gravy. But we didn't get a vote on that. Pass me a biscuit, would you? And the gravy."

Buddy didn't ask about the phone calls. Waiting seemed like the polite thing to do, particularly since they were enjoying the food so much.

He didn't have to ask. "Thanks for the breakfast, Buddy. I sure enjoyed it. Real home cooking would be better, but this is pretty good," Elmer said. He wiped his mouth with his napkin and checked a gravy spot on the front of his shirt. Pointing to the spot he said, "I did that on purpose. It'll make everybody jealous over at the home." He grinned at Buddy and Bill. "I guess you want to hear about our phone calls this week."

Bill said, "I'm glad we had a reason to call. Talking to those guys made me feel good. Nothing ever happens at the home that makes a day worth getting up for. But knowing we were goin' to be calling someone every day made the whole week pass a lot faster."

Elmer said, "It's kind of surprising, all of those guys on the list are still alive. Trouble is, they all wanted to talk about their ailments. Hell, we've got enough of our own. We don't need to hear anyone else's bad news. We won't tell you all of those stories, but I will say three of them are in pretty bad shape."

Bill interrupted. "That's neither here nor there. Fact is, out of the five, four of 'em remembered Sonny. They all said he was one of the best old boys they ever worked with."

Elmer nodded. He sat forward to pass along his next bit. "John Sagelin had a real useful piece of information; course it took me a long time to get it out of him. He always was kind of close-mouthed. Anyway, he still lives up in Wichita County, close to Holliday. He said Sonny quit working the rigs and started pumping. Said that was in the early nineteen sixties sometime."

Bill leaned toward Buddy. "Now I hope this next part won't upset you. He told us that Sonny and Martha Clay lived together. Everyone thought they was married. But John knew different. He said she's still alive, living in Wichita Falls."

Elmer nodded again, as if urging Bill along—not that Bill could see the cue. Then when Bill paused for breath, Elmer interrupted, "He didn't recall what year, but he said Sonny died when he was in his seventies. He said he thought it was nineteen eighty something, said the funeral was real nice."

Buddy sat back, slumped against his chair. Elmer didn't seem to notice. He said, "If you want all the facts, the next step would be to see if you can get a hold of Martha Clay. If her mind is still working, she should be able to tell you the whole story."

Bill reached out a hand and found Buddy's shoulder. He patted it. "I sure hope this didn't upset you, son. But you did say you wanted to know."

"I did. I'm not upset; I'm just surprised."

"You know, there's no explaining the things people do if you don't know their whole story. We shouldn't judge old Sonny. Not at this late date. Gotta remember too, everyone said he was the best they ever worked with—real smart and real patient."

Buddy said, "You're right about not judging. I can think of three or four reasons at home why he might have wanted to disappear. I appreciate y'all for doing the detective work."

The next day he and Delta went back to Lubbock and parked the trailer at the county hospital. Sometime that night, after staring at the ceiling and squinting at the light sliding in through the trailer's little bedroom window for what seemed like a long time, he made a decision.

The next morning, Buddy said, "I've decided to go to Wichita Falls tomorrow and see Martha Clay." He was talking from the bedroom; Delta was sitting a few feet away in the trailer's kitchen-living area. "I called information and got her number. Then I talked to her yesterday while you were taking a nap. She sounded surprised, but I don't think she was upset. She said to come on over and we'd talk. She lives in a retirement community. Made sure to tell me it wasn't a nursing home."

He stepped into the kitchen because so far he had conducted his side of the conversation out of sight, like a ventriloquist practicing a new routine. He took a big breath and fiddled with the pickup keys and checked his billfold. Finally he started out the door, saying, "I'm going to run a couple of errands..." Then a second later he went back inside and said, "Unless you just want to go, I'll go over there tomorrow by myself."

"To Wichita Falls?"

"Yes, I want to get this taken care of, off my mind."

"I have things to read and there's a park close. I'll stay here and if I want to go anywhere else, I'll call a cab."

He tried to get a good breath, then said, "Yeah, good idea. I'll get an early start in the morning."

He drew another big breath. This time it came more easily.

Buddy was up by half past six the next morning, rummaging around. He talked all the time he was putting socks and underwear and a shirt in his small overnight bag, not asking Delta any questions, just commenting on the weather and so forth, mostly to distract himself. Delta had made coffee and then stayed in the living area. She may or may not have heard anything he said. It didn't matter, he couldn't seem to shut up.

Overnight bag in hand, he took a gulp of the coffee she'd poured in a thermal cup. "Thanks for this. I'll get something to eat down the road a ways." He looked around and didn't know what he might be looking for. "Okay, I guess I'm ready." He turned toward the door, then came back and hugged her.

He had started backing the pickup out, then he stopped because Delta was outside, waving to get his attention. She handed him his cell phone and sunglasses. He said, "Guess I'm a little distracted."

"In that case, be extra careful. I'll be right here if you need to call."

"Don't worry. I'll be okay." He backed a few feet, then stopped again. He rolled down his window and said, "Delta, I love you." She'd already opened the door to the trailer. He doubted if she heard.

Nearing Wichita Falls, the dread that had lodged in his stomach spread to his chest and shoulders. The drive he should have made in a little over four hours took closer to six, mostly due to his making three bathroom stops. Next time he'd remember not to drink so much coffee. He didn't dwell on the pain in his back, but stopping to walk around helped that.

So it was close to 1:30 by the time he checked into a motel on the outskirts of Wichita. About twenty more minutes and he made the turn at the driveway to Rolling Hills Retirement Homes. Just turning the steering wheel taxed his strength. Driving slowly, he located 221 Hillside Lane. It wasn't anything like that nursing home. Each of the apartments sat back from a postage stamp sized area of ground cover behind a low fence. He opened the gate and noticed a pot of bright pink petunias on each side of the porch. A plate below the doorbell button confirmed it was Martha Clay's apartment. So far, so good. He wiped his palms on his pants and pressed the button.

A short, slender woman with white hair greeted him with a smile that reminded him of Delta. He said, "Miss Clay?"

She said, "I can tell you're Buddy. You are your dad made over. Come on in. Please call me Martha."

She offered iced tea, to which he said yes. When she returned to the living room from the little kitchen he could see from where he sat, she brought a tray with the tea, some small sandwiches, and cookies. The scent of cinnamon followed her from the kitchen. She said, "I thought you might not have eaten on the way over here."

He worked his way through a couple of sandwiches and three cookies and then leaned back against the couch cushion. How he'd finally relaxed, he didn't know, but this place felt homey. Even though the living room was small, nothing about it suggested an institution.

Martha said, "There's a lot I'd love to tell you and I want to know all about you, but you probably have some questions. So I'll let you go first."

While she'd been talking, he'd noticed a picture on the end table. She and his dad laughing, dressed in matching western shirts. She had changed little from when it had been taken except her hair was dark then and she wasn't wearing glasses. His dad looked just the way he remembered him, but happier than he ever recalled. "I wondered about how you met and when."

She leaned toward him and said, "That picture was taken a few months after we met. We'd gone to a rodeo." She reached for it and handed it to him. "It was 1953, I think. I was working at First National Bank in Wichita. He came into the bank and I helped him open an account. Filling out the forms, he mentioned he was living at Holliday. I lived there too."

She paused and closed her eyes for a second. "We started talking about one of the cafes in Holliday that made a good chicken-fried steak. I don't know what made me so bold, but I told him that even if I did say so, and shouldn't, I made the best chicken-fried steak in Archer County, maybe all of Texas."

Buddy watched as she told the story, her gestures and lively expressions told him she'd visited that memory lots of times before.

"Without missing a beat, Sonny frowned and said, 'Ma'am, I'm the official judge in that contest.'

"I said, 'What contest is that, Mr. Bell?'

"'The contest that awards the title Best Chicken-Fried Steak in Texas. You can't make that claim unless I award the title. The official competition is next Friday night in Holliday. If you'd like to enter, just put your address and telephone number on this entry form.'

"He handed me a blank piece of paper. I was so tickled, I did it. That was the best line anyone had ever used to get a date with me."

Buddy laughed along with her. "That sounds like the things I used to hear him pull on those roughnecks he'd take under his wing."

"He was a good man who never had a bad word for anyone. I couldn't have been happier with anyone else in the world. What else do you wonder about?"

He wasn't able to find the right way to ask, so he shrugged. It just didn't seem right to make her remember his dying, however it happened.

Maybe she read his mind. "I imagine you want to know about his death."

"Yes, if you don't mind."

"It was February, 1982. We'd been together nearly thirty years by then. He'd taken his retirement a few years before, and we'd been planning to travel some. I still have all the brochures, places we were going to see. The Grand Canyon was first on the list. Then one morning, we already had our hotel reservations, one morning I got up and found him dead in his recliner. He had had a mild heart attack a couple of years before. Then that day, he'd had another one, a big one."

By the time she finished tears trickled down her cheeks. "Excuse me," she said, "I'll be right back."

He heard her in the other room blowing her nose. Heart attack. He never dreamed it would be that. None of his own symptoms matched heart trouble.

She came back to her chair, smiling again, carrying a photo album. "Sometimes it's hard." She took a loud breath. "Don't worry about those tears. I wouldn't want to forget. I'd like you to tell me about yourself, and then after that, you might want to take a bit to look at these pictures."

The things he told her turned out to be lots more than he intended, mostly because she seemed genuinely interested and encouraged him with questions and comments.

Her phone rang and when she went to answer, he began leafing through the album. She returned to her chair, and said she'd arranged the pictures by years, with the earliest at the front. Some included other people, and his dad was in almost all of them. Martha must have been the photographer. She sat quietly as he studied the pictures.

As the years passed, they were visible on his father's face in the way that laughter and hard work etch themselves permanently. If anything, Buddy thought he'd grown more handsome than he recalled. Even in the last pages, as he passed sixty, the photos showed a man who stood erect and looked at the camera straight on, his eyes full of light and life. Wishing he'd known him longer, Buddy felt tears on his face. He fished for his handkerchief. Apparently he'd left home without it. "May I use your bathroom, please?"

He took his time letting the sadness spill out, then rinsed his face, and blew his nose.

In the living room again, he said, "I know you have other things to do, so I'll be going. I really appreciate your time. It's helped me a lot to know what happened to my dad. I guess I'll never know why my mother lied to us."

She smiled, but didn't say more than what she'd already told him. "I hope you'll come back to visit again. Bring your wife. I love having company." As she followed him to the gate, she said, "Thank you for coming. This has been a good day for me."

That night, alone in the motel, Buddy lay across the bed and finished the crying he'd made himself stop at Martha Clay's. Later, after waking to use the bathroom, his heart raced when he saw blood in his urine. The rest of the night, he changed positions fitfully, but eventually slept and woke near nine.

The first thing Buddy said when he came in from Wichita Falls, after he hugged Delta, was, "I haven't had anything to eat but a package of peanut butter crackers since the middle of the morning. Let's go eat."

It took him quite a while to get around to talking about his trip. First, he studied the menu at Mitchell's Restaurant. He could have memorized it by the time he finally ordered catfish. Then he said, "The Four Sixes Ranch looked mighty dry when I passed through there."

He heard the words he was saying, and could even see himself, as if he was observing from a distance. He tore a roll into pieces and stared at the result.

Without looking away from the pile of scraps he'd made, he said, "I'm not sure where to start to tell about Martha Clay and her story." He looked everywhere except directly at Delta while he talked. Then the waiter brought their order. That delayed the story for a while longer.

He fiddled with his food and started eating French fries. Then, as if he'd been in the middle of a sentence, he said, "Okay, I could see why he liked her. She's a real nice lady—still sharp, and you can tell she was pretty when she was young. She doesn't look eighty. He was older than she was. She said they never married because he didn't want to get a divorce and upset my mother any more than he already had. She said not a week went by that he didn't talk about us kids, sometimes feeling bad about leaving us, other times just wondering how we turned out.

Maybe she might have said that just to make me feel better. I don't know.

"There were pictures in her apartment of him and of the two of them. He looked just like I remember him. She said I look a lot like him." He stopped talking and worked on getting bones out of his fish. When there was nothing else he could do to the fish, he looked up and said, "When she told me how he died, heart attack, as they were getting ready for a vacation, I felt sorry for her."

"What year was that?" He knew Delta well enough to know she asked to give him a break from trying to tell something that was so emotional for him. It was good she did; otherwise he'd have had to admit he was close to crying, again.

"It was nineteen eighty-two. He would have been sixty-nine." He ate the last forkful of rice on his plate, slowly. "As sorry as I was to hear about him dying that way, I'm glad he didn't die in a nursing home, or even in a hospital. And I'm glad he was with Martha Clay. That woman said she still misses him every day. She loved him."

He stared at the boy clearing dishes at the next table. "She's a woman who laughs a lot. Nobody at our house, Mama or the girls, ever joked around with Daddy. I don't know how it turned out that way. Mama was grim most of the time. Even with the two girls, if she was laughing and talking with them, I'd get the feeling that underneath, she was unhappy. It doesn't surprise me he left."

He added sweetener to his iced tea, stirred it for a long time, and then said, "Martha Clay didn't steal him from us. He'd been alone working up in Wyoming before they ever met."

He reached for Delta's hand. "When he died, he'd been happy, a lot of it because of her. A real sweet woman. She reminded me of you." He drank some of the tea. All the thoughts he'd had the past few days, the fears he entertained last night came in a rush. He set his glass down, shook his head as if he could find a clear way to steer through them.

When he noticed Delta watching him, he said, "I'm glad he never had to be in a nursing home."

On the way back from Wichita Falls, he'd thought about how to tell Delta he probably had something that would kill him, that was making him feel so bad and so old. Then he decided maybe it was nothing serious, that he was acting like Mama, only seeing the worst possible. Maybe he was getting as crazy as she did. That would be an even worse thing. The only answer that came to him was that whatever it was, she'd understand. He could count on Delta.

She said, "I'm glad you visited her. It'll do you good to know, help make you peaceful about him, and about yourself."

On the way back to the trailer, neither one of them spoke. But Delta moved close to him and put her hand on his back, and left it there. When they got inside, he said, "I need to tell you something else."

He started slowly, but kept on.

Across the Vermilion Border

I am hitting my daughter; first time in her life, my life. The thought
slams across Sandra's mind just after her hand detaches itself
from her volition, and bolts across the space between them to
collide with Tiffany's face. *Tiffany, the name her father chose, his
favorite name, he said. He never said why.*

That left hand, the one that Sandra sees acting without
her will, wears a turquoise ring, intended to cover the pale band
left bare when she threw her wedding ring in the Dumpster the
day after the divorce.

The delicate-featured fifteen year-old face, from which
"You bitch—You want me to hate men like you do—You can't
keep me from talking to him and you can't make me stop seeing
him—And I'll have sex when I want to" had just spewed, twists
into a caricature of surprise and fear. Sandra has no idea how
her own face looks, perhaps as unfamiliar as the hand.

Another thought telegraphs across the ocean between
intention and awareness. *I taught her how to call Children's Protective
when she was twelve. She will. I'll lose my job.*

And then, that hand, tingling with impact, bears blood. A
dark red ribbon ties the ring finger to the wrist, binding them
into a weapon that has just destroyed so much she worked so
long to accomplish.

The pressure pulsing in her ears drops, descends to her
stomach. She draws a deep breath; she cannot allow herself to
vomit now. But the sight of her daughter's face closes her eyes.
Not a ribbon, but a bright red stream flows down from the right
side of her only child's top lip. Blood falls in syrupy globules
from Tiffany's chin. *I did that.* Blood falls onto the leftover pizza,

onto the pale birch-topped kitchen table, drop after enormous drop.

Tiffany has never been spanked, much less slapped, and certainly never physically injured at the hands of an adult. Sandra would have reported any teacher who so much as threatened to lay a hand on her daughter, the child with the perfect face and the too wise eyes. She would have stalked and killed anyone who molested her only child. If her ex-husband had ever focused on their child the barely disguised anger that fueled his surly silences, Sandra would have left, fled and taken Tiffany to another state or a foreign country as she often dreamed of doing.

None of those things had ever happened. Instead, everyone conspired to adore Tiffany, the perfect child.

The fear and surprise on Tiffany's face disappears into anger. People have always told Sandra that Tiffany doesn't resemble her father at all. But now, a glare that carries his mark focuses a force on her mother that flings up a boundary and keeps Sandra from reaching to comfort her.

"Hold that on your mouth to stop the bleeding." She points to a kitchen towel on the back of a chair. "Be still. I'll get ice." Tiffany doesn't move, doesn't speak. "Do it now," Sandra says, louder than she intends, in the tone she uses to separate eighth-grade boys fighting in the lunchroom. The refrigerator door's domestic décor mocks her and her shaking hands—schedules for track meets, pictures of Tiffany in her track uniform, a drawing Sandra saved that Tiffany made when she was five—things a normal mother would treasure. She focuses on getting ice. The smell of overripe cantaloupe rises into the freezer from the refrigerator below.

In seconds, Sandra whirls back toward the table with ice cubes wrapped in a kitchen towel. *Did I close the freezer?* As she reaches toward Tiffany, the girl twitches, almost cowers. Her shoulders shake as she sobs soundlessly. Tears mixed with blood drip onto her blouse.

"This should stop the blood. It probably looks worse than it is," Sandra says.

A phone's ring tone startles them both. Tiffany's. Sandra hears a wet intake of breath, feels Tiffany's shoulders straighten, a reflex. A phone. How it started. Minutes ago, years ago. "Don't move. It's mine. Ignore it," Sandra says. "We have to stop the bleeding."

She lifts the kitchen towel from Tiffany's face. Worse. As soon as the pressure is removed, the bleeding increases. Swelling makes a distorted sneer of her child's mouth which, when her braces come off next month, would have been even more perfect than before. *Do something. Say something—you're the adult.*

"I'm taking you to the Minor Emergency Clinic. Press this against your lip. Go to the car." *Disaster preparedness for teachers. Issue directions in short sentences.* "I have to get my purse. I'll be right there." *How can I explain to a doctor? Truth will be easiest.* She'll be reported, but her child will know she didn't lie. Sandra brought Tiffany up to always tell the truth and to consider the results of both actions and words. Words—she'd been so panicked by the message she read, she can't even recall all the words she had said to her daughter. But every syllable Tiffany uttered had burned into Sandra's heart the minute she heard them.

The street sign says Fairway Boulevard. Three blocks from their house and Sandra can't recall traveling any distance at all. She makes a right turn and joins the evening commuter traffic streaming off the Hansford Loop. Two stops in one block. Tiffany stares out the passenger side window, her hand and the makeshift ice bag to her face, her shoulders rigid. *Less blood now. But the cut has to be repaired. There will be a scar.* Traffic creeps forward toward the invisible barrier that separates their residential area from Elm Park's commercial district. Six more blocks. *No turning back now.* Even if Sandra wanted to go home, reversing direction would take more attention than she trusts herself to muster.

She had picked the phone up from the kitchen table when she heard the "thunk" signaling an arriving text message. Probably her sister Brenda, the stay at home mom who escaped her own tedium by texting Sandra several times each day. "Go today to Planned Parenthood. They'll do a test. J" Who? One of her students? A prank?

Another "thunk." The next message read "It'll be k. UR on my mind all the time. I luv U Jess." The sender's number was blocked.

From the hallway, "Mom, have you seen my phone?"

Sandra handed her the phone. "I thought it was mine."

She watched Tiffany swipe it with an index finger and scan its screen. "Who is Jess?" Sandra asked. Her own voice sounded as if it came from far away.

"What?"

"You heard me. Who's Jess?" She held back the other questions.

"A guy."

"Where do you know him from?" At least Tiffany hadn't lied and said Jess was a girlfriend.

"I don't know. The mall I guess." She punched something on the phone, waited, then swiped across the screen again. Her eyes narrowed. "You snooped my messages."

Pressure built, clogging Sandra's ears. "Don't you dare stand there accusing me. I wasn't snooping. I heard a message signal. Thought it was mine. Have you been seeing this Jess?" Her chest constricted as she said the name. Probably some twenty-year old predator. Something about Tiffany's eyes made her look older, ripe.

"Remember, I'm not allowed to date." Mocking her mother with facts.

"I remember. Do you?"

Before Sandra could speak again, Tiffany, louder now, as if she had a righteous cause, said, "I talk to guys even if I can't go out. Lots of guys have my number."

Words from *Adolescent Psychology for Teachers* bounced inside Sandra's skull. *Teenage oppositional behavior, testing limits, part of normal development.* In the past two months, small incidents— avoiding homework, whining about doing her few assigned household chores, delaying bedtime, getting up late, cigarette smoke on her clothes—had become frequent. And there had been the day she and Kelly ditched school. The attendance office notified Sandra at nine a.m. She took a sick day and roamed the mall until she found the two girls trying on high heels in the shoe department at Dillard's. Sandra had responded firmly and, she thought, reasonably to that and each of the other issues as they arose. Tiffany had apologized; they negotiated a later bedtime and different chores; and the truancy cost her television and phone privileges for a month. *Appropriate adult responses.* Sandra had said nothing to her ex-husband about Tiffany's behavior—it was normal.

But lying…. "You're lucky it was me and not your father who saw that."

"Daddy would never pry. He respects me, treats me like an adult."

"Every moment together is bliss, I'm sure." Sandra heard her own sarcasm too late to stop it.

Another thunk. Tiffany turned the phone over and checked its screen, then put it in her jeans pocket. She challenged Sandra with a stare and said, "I'm going. Meet Kelly at the track. Run some laps."

She'd started running, cross country and long distance, just after the divorce, at the suggestion of the counselor. He'd said the vomiting and weight loss that started when they separated was Tiffany's unconscious attempt to gain control. Apparently his diagnosis was correct. She had made the junior high track team and stopped vomiting and losing weight. Now that she was a sophomore, she already had college scholarship opportunities as a result. Long lean legs, lithe body; she was built for running.

"No, you're going to stay right here. You're going to explain why this Jess is telling you go to Planned Parenthood."

"A joke." Her face flushed, the color of a lie.

"What kind of test? STDs? Pregnancy? Have you…." Sandra expected another lie.

Instead, silence stood like a barrier between them. Finally, Tiffany said quietly, "What if I have? It's my business. I know what I'm doing."

"You think you do. You have no idea."

"You thought you did," Tiffany said.

Sandra felt the words like a slap across her own face.

Tiffany, when she was twelve, had asked Sandra why they never celebrated their wedding anniversary. Sandra's answer, though not a lie, something about it being too near Christmas to have another special occasion, avoided the fact. Tiffany hadn't pressed for more, but Sandra had no doubt she did the math. All she had to do was subtract her own age from her mother's to know she was born when Sandra was sixteen. They had married a month before Tiffany's birth.

Tiffany turned to leave the room. "I'm going. I'll be home later."

"No, you're not. You're grounded. Give me that phone. I'm keeping it for two months this time." She was talking to her daughter's back.

In a quick motion, so smooth it might have been practiced, Tiffany whirled toward Sandra and threw the telephone across the room, a low hard pitch that barely missed Sandra and hit the baseboard in the corner. Its screen blinked alternately black and blue.

She grabbed at her daughter, caught her tee shirt and her right arm, jerked hard. "That was the last mistake you're going to make with me. No phone, and you're grounded, including after school activities until further notice. I have reached my limit." Sandra wrestled to control her breathing.

Tiffany stood still, not resisting. She glared directly at her mother as she spoke. "It won't matter. I'm going to tell Daddy I'm coming to live with him. He'll understand. I'll make sure he does." Roaring in Sandra's ears baffled the sound. Tiffany's challenge seemed to come from the far bank of a wild river.

Sandra screamed, a loud wail that Tiffany backed away from. Sandra jerked her close again, gripping both shoulders. She shouted, "You think you're grown up. I guess you think you're in love, too. Having sex at your age!" The part of her that watched from a distance saw a mother clutching a near-grown daughter, pulling her back from the edge of a dark pit. "You think you're an adult—you're nothing but a spoiled, stupid slut. You'll turn up pregnant—married at sixteen."

That's when Tiffany had wrenched one shoulder free, screamed those hateful words.

That's when Sandra hit her. How it started and they ended up on their way to a place they had never been before.

Honking. The Ford pickup in front of them moves forward a few feet. The driver behind honks again. Sandra looks at the driver in her rearview mirror, a pale, grim-faced woman in a hurry; or is that her own reflection? She inches forward to occupy the few feet the pickup vacated. She looks briefly at Tiffany's profile. The flow of blood must have slowed; the towel is no redder and nothing is dripping from her chin.

She doesn't mind the slowness of the traffic now that hemorrhage doesn't seem imminent. This stop light will eventually change; they will cross Barnett Road, the final main artery between them and the clinic. They will wait some more. A doctor will appear and perform some medical acts to remedy the bleeding and restore Tiffany's beauty. And then the story will be told, and she will be labeled an abusive parent and will lose her job. No hurry; it is all arranged.

She's never loved her job and wouldn't mind being free of the responsibility of corralling eighth graders, trying to teach them art and simultaneously hold them back from the impulsive acts prompted by pubertal hormones. But she worked hard to be able to have a job that used her talent and supported them both.

She finished high school by correspondence, went to college part-time for eight years, struggled to pay for child care, and did everything a good parent should do—PTA, soccer, all of it. For more than twelve years, she stayed with the boy who turned into the silent grim man she eventually hated. She stayed because he adored Tiffany, who followed him everywhere when he was home, and because at sixteen, Sandra had promised marriage would be forever. It hadn't been his fault any more than hers. They had been young and full of hormones and had no thoughts of contraceptives.

She tries to recall how the two of them had looked back then, but can't recognize the image from her memory. All she sees are a girl and boy with soft, unformed faces and young warm bodies.

When her husband left, she fought for and won custody of their only child, with weekend and vacation visits for Tiffany at her father's. Finally, the pall of gloom he carried no longer darkened Sandra's days. She even had a savings account now and money enough for nice clothes for the two of them. In the three years since the divorce, she had relearned how to laugh. Until the past two or three months, when Tiffany started acting like a teenager, life had been better than she had ever expected.

The Wichita Regional Hospital Urgent Care and Minor Emergency Center waiting room shelters a crowd, mostly women and children. Some are coughing; some sit quietly, intermittently watching television sets anchored high on the white walls. No one else in the room clutches a bloody kitchen towel.

"Sit there," Sandra says and points to a chair near the glass enclosure where the admission clerk waits. No injury or illness in Tiffany's life had required emergency care; a butterfly closure sealed the only cut that ever bled more than a second; ear infections resolved without incident; no seizures; no fractures; no asthma attacks with frantic pleas for oxygen and bronchodilators. There will be papers to sign, explanations to give. *What language do they speak in this foreign territory?*

"Is she still bleeding?" The woman in the glass cage asks, before Sandra can speak. "If she is, bring her in the back and I'll get your information there."

The exam room offers Frozen murals on two walls, no television. Tiffany lies on the exam table now, holding a clean towel to her face, silent. The admission woman leaves them together after collecting insurance numbers and identification. The nurse who supplied the towel disappears. *I should say something, do what a good mother would do.* The room they were in could have been miles from the waiting area. No sound enters or exits as the two of them wait. Sandra sits in an uncomfortable plastic chair, closes her eyes, and leans her head back against the wall, into the Frozen lap of Anna, the optimist. *I will get in the car and drive as far as I can. Another state, maybe Mexico or Canada.* She sees herself alone in the car on a dark road.

The door squeaks as the nurse returns. "The doctor will be in soon. Tiffany, let me check to see if the bleeding has stopped," she said. "Not quite. Are you dizzy or do you feel faint?" She wraps a blood pressure cuff around Tiffany's left arm and watches as the machine declares an answer. "Blood pressure's okay, one ten over seventy. Pulse a little fast, ninety." She pats Tiffany on the arm, glances toward Sandra. Before leaving, she places a cold pack in a fresh towel in Tiffany's hand. "Just keep holding this on your lip." The used towel stays behind, a lump of Chinese red, evidence on a stainless steel tray.

Another squeak of the door and the doctor enters. He nods to Sandra and says to Tiffany, "I'm Dr. Lee. I'm going to take a look at this and see what's what, and then I'll need some information."

He puts on a pair of magnifying glasses and pulls an exam light near. He takes the towel from Tiffany's hand and bends close to her face. "There is a single irregularly shaped laceration on the right upper lip approximately one point five centimeters long and point five centimeters deep. Bleeding appears to be slowing. The cut has to be sutured or it will heal slowly and unevenly." He sounds as if he is dictating notes for a chart. He steps back and speaks to both of them. "The problem is that the laceration crosses the vermilion border. This line here." He demonstrates by pointing to himself. "The line where face turns to lip. Different types of tissue. Regardless of how carefully the edges are pulled together, there will be a scar."

Sandra nods. *What should I say?* Tiffany whimpers.

Dr. Lee steps away to a counter where Tiffany's chart lies. Sandra stands and moves near the exam table. *A scar on my daughter's perfect face.* Tiffany's eyes seem focused on a distant point, somewhere far away from this room, away from Sandra.

The doctor proceeds briskly through questions and answers about past medical history—all normal, no allergies, immunizations up to date—attending to the chart, making checkmarks, not looking at either of them. He pauses and looks directly at Tiffany. "How did the injury occur?"

Sandra holds her breath, rehearsing the words in her mind. *I did it. I hit her.* Should she explain that at the moment she did it, the hand that struck Tiffany was not actually hers, that for a brief second, she had not regretted whatever had pushed her past the edge? *Please don't report me to Child Protective. I'll lose my job. I'll lose my daughter.* Would anyone here understand that everyone has a limit?

Tiffany lifts the cold compress. "Running. I'm a runner."

Sounds distorted. Sandra resists an urge to nod in the doctor's direction, to imply that the words bear truth. Instead she exhales slowly and stands completely still.

"Where were you when this happened?" he asks Tiffany, but Sandra feels him staring at her. *How does he know? Does it show on my face?*

"Home," Tiffany says, clearer this time.

"The phone." Tiffany pauses, takes the towel away from her lip, stares at the blood. "She always tells me to be still when texting. I hit the door. My braces."

No glance passes between Tiffany and Sandra, no signal of collusion. Sandra receives the lie as a solution, a gift, really. Not an intentional purchase on her part.

The threat of a polyester-suited CPS investigator snapping photos of Tiffany's face recedes; the image of a school-district Human Resources functionary explaining the careful verbiage her terminal evaluation would contain evaporates. *What did that cost?*

"Did you fall?"

Tiffany nods.

"I'll need to look you over to see if there are any other injuries." He turns to Sandra with a glance that lingers, a frown line between his eyes. "And we have to decide what you want to do about repairing the laceration."

He looks at his watch. "We can do it here, safely; I've done some plastics work. I have the time right now. Or we can send you over to the ED at the main hospital and get the plastic surgeon on call to do the repair. Either way, she'll have to have some light IV anesthesia for a few minutes during the suturing. I'll have to call for an anesthetist from the main hospital."

Before Sandra can think, Tiffany says, "Do it here." *Muffled, speaking from an entirely different country.*

"Regardless, there'll be a scar. I can't promise there won't be."

"I should call her father. I'll be right back." *I don't know what to say.*

In the hallway, facing the exit sign, she manages to punch in his number on her phone, watching her alien hand again as it shakes. After five unanswered rings, his voice mail responds. Sandra leaves a message. "Tiffany had a cut that has to be sutured. We're at the Urgent Care on Eighty-eighth Street. I wanted you to know. No need for you to come. She'll call you later tonight. It's about six p.m. now."

If he gets the message any time soon, he will come. No doubt. Almost from her birth, Tiffany had played the part of baby girl to her dad's doting father. Since the divorce, two weekends a month, two months in the summer, and alternate holidays, he has focused entirely on her every whim. *It's good she knows we both love her.*

Sandra pushes the squeaky door open and enters the exam room; the doctor and the nurse turn toward her. *Were they asking Tiffany more questions? Are they suspicious?* She looks toward Tiffany, who looks away. "Your dad's phone went to messages. I left one telling him where we are and said you'd call him after we get home."

"He's not coming?" a child's voice asks.

"If he gets the message, I'm sure he will. But he didn't answer."

"I need to talk to him." Now Tiffany sounds a little defiant, normal.

The doctor says, "We'll need to draw some blood." He looks down at the chart, up at Tiffany. "When was your last menstrual period?"

"Not sure," she says. "A runner."

Sandra says, "Not always regular. Athletes."

"It's routine before anesthesia or other meds. We'll do a test, just to be safe."

Sandra looks at Tiffany's face, thinks she sees something. Hopes it's her imagination. The doctor explains that they will move Tiffany to a procedure room nearby and he'll suture the wound—that's what he calls the thing she did to her daughter— as soon as the anesthetist arrives. It will only take a few minutes.

She closes her eyes and leans back in the waiting room chair. Pushing all thoughts of escape to foreign territory from her mind, she focuses on a spot on the opposite wall, just as she had in labor with Tiffany. A movement at the doorway of the waiting room calls her attention. The doctor stands there beckoning. She follows him, waiting for him to speak. At another door, he stops and tells her the suturing is completed and there will be only a very small scar.

"Right now, because there's edema, the lip won't look as nice as it will when that resolves. In a couple of weeks, there will be only a hairline scar and over time, it will fade a lot." He pauses as if he might expect a question or a compliment.

"You'll tell me what to do until it heals, when to get the sutures out?"

"Definitely. Written instructions. She'll be clear enough to go home in twenty or thirty minutes." He busies himself with the chart. Then he says, "By the way, her tests were all fine— CBC, no anemia; negative pregnancy test."

"Can I go to her?"

He nods and points in the room to a curtained area on his left.

Sandra edges the curtain back to peek. Tiffany's eyes are closed. Even with the bandage, she's beautiful. Movement of her eyes beneath the lids tells Sandra her daughter's not asleep.

Sandra pushes the curtain along the track in the ceiling and moves next to the bed. "You awake?"

Tiffany nods and opens her eyes. "Are they through? Can I go?"

"Soon. Your dad called. He'll be here any minute."

"I'll wait for him," Tiffany says.

Sandra stares at the oddly shaped bulk of the lip and the small dressing topping it like a dollop of whipped cream. "The doctor says this will be healed in a couple of weeks and the scar will be tiny and will fade."

Tiffany shrugs. "Maybe."

"I'm sorry this happened," Sandra says.

No sound from her daughter. Sandra turns away, looks for and can't find a chair.

"When Daddy comes…I'm going home with him. You tell him I can live with him now."

"You won't be happy there… I know." *Now I know the price.*

A nurse comes into the cubicle, looks at the dressing, checks Tiffany's blood pressure, and leaves, all without a word. Tiffany rolls to her right side, her back to her mother.

In the waiting area again, outside the minor surgery room, a shadow crosses the page Sandra's staring at, pretending to read. She looks up, not surprised to see Tiffany's father standing above her, hands clenched at his sides. Still grim, as always. He says, "What happened? Why did they have to put her to sleep if it's just a cut? What are you not telling me?"

"It's a cut on her lip that wouldn't stop bleeding. Not big, but in a difficult place. So they needed to give her an anesthetic while they sutured it. The doctor said everything was fine and the scar will be very small. She'll be dismissed soon." She doesn't mention Tiffany's plan. *Let her tell him.*

He paces back and forth in front of her, one side of the small area to the other, two full circuits. "How did it happen? Where were you?"

"At home with her." *Where were you?*

"Where is she? She needs to know I'm here."

Sandra points to the door to the curtained room.

He squints and focuses on the door.

She trails behind, able only to see his back, the shoulders of the high school Golden Gloves champ now hunched by habit into the wary stance of an old heavyweight. He treads like a man in a minefield.

Tiffany reaches for his hand as soon as she sees him. "Daddy, take me home with you, please."

Sandra stands at the foot of the bed, watching his face, fascinated by his effort to create a reassuring smile for his daughter, and waiting for more interrogation; he never failed to suspect her. For once he would be right.

"Are you okay, baby?" he asks.

Tiffany nods and sniffles.

"Your mother said this was an accident at home. Is that the truth? An accident?"

Tiffany nods again. "Take me with you, Daddy. She says it's okay."

"Sure, baby. Of course."

After about thirty minutes of blood pressure checks, papers signed, instructions given, Tiffany is on the way to being dismissed. It had seemed to Sandra like thirty hours, the whole time in the heat of her ex-husband's suspicious stare.

Tiffany's father pushes her, in a wheelchair, toward the exit. A nurse follows. Sandra walks slowly behind the three of them, managing to continue forward by concentrating on each step.

Talking to the nurse, he says, "I'll have to bring my car around to the back here to pick her up. Will you stay with her?" The nurse nods and glances briefly at Sandra.

Tiffany lets go of her father's hand. She speaks in a muffled, little girl voice, "I'll be fine, Daddy."

The nurse asks Sandra to watch Tiffany, says she'll be back in a minute. Sandra stands behind the wheelchair and smoothes her child's hair.

"Mother, Daddy will bring me to get my stuff tomorrow or this weekend." A cold determined statement, a challenge. "And you're wrong; Jess and I are in love."

"You can come home whenever you're ready." Sandra looks at her beautiful daughter, sees her as she was and as she hopes she will become.

The nurse returns and hands Sandra a plastic bag containing the bloody kitchen towel.

Holding the bag at an awkward angle away from her body, she gathers her purse and the discharge papers. She sees her ex-husband parking near the exit. "There's your dad. I'm going out the other way. Taking care of the bill. I'll pay."

The Woman with a Miniature Donkey

Sunlight glinting off the window of the engine on the train track two miles away struck me in my right eye. An omen. It was a signal I should see the light, brighten up. All the years we were kids, my sister and I slept in this room in this house on what used to be a farm. And as far back as I could recall, trains passing on that track brought me messages. Something good was going to come my way soon. Maybe it would come by rail, or I'd meet it while clacking along at the steady pace of a train going somewhere, secure in a tiny, snug compartment.

Maybe not. Maybe I'll miss whatever's coming my way because I'm spending my time cleaning up after my sister.

Taking two final sweaters from the top drawer, I pushed both into the black plastic bag at my feet. One emptied, three drawers and four rooms to go. I slammed the drawer closed. The Mason jar on the dresser's top, holding one dried yellow rose, toppled to its side. In the process of righting the jar, my hand gathered dust, leaving a trail across the chest's top. I said, and it wasn't a whisper, "What were you so busy doing you couldn't dust now and then?"

How ridiculous, talking to Margaret. What was left of her, the cremated remains, had occupied the passenger seat of my car since Tuesday when I picked them up at the funeral home. Her out there, me in here. It didn't matter. I went on talking, "You'll get where you're going soon enough. First I have to clean up the mess you left."

Then I promised myself I was through talking to my dead sister, at least speaking aloud, if for no other reason than it seemed like a symptom. The only difference was that I actually uttered my thoughts rather than keeping them to myself as I usually did. I read somewhere that highly creative people often talk to themselves. But still, I wonder if it's common to wait until the age of fifty-eight to begin.

I managed to keep that vow for about half an hour, until I opened the third drawer from the top. Squatting would be uncomfortable, so I dumped the contents on the bed, planning to sort from there. The first thing that fell out, the flannel pajamas I gave her for Christmas two years ago, had never even been unfolded, just taken out of the box. Pins still held them in a perfect rectangle wrapped in a single layer of white tissue paper. Then under that, six plain white panties and a new white bra, all with price tags dangling. Okay, if she wanted to save her decent underwear for some unnamed later time, I guess that's her business. But as I lifted the garter belt that had fallen on top, I couldn't help it. I said, "What? Did you think they'd come back in style? You're wrong. They won't, not since they invented pantyhose. Not if you're a normal sixty-year-old woman who only goes to work and the grocery store and lives twelve miles from the nearest town."

No answer. No surprise. She never was one to explain herself. To tell the truth, I always admired that confidence. One time when we were kids, about ten and twelve, Daddy had us out working with him. Back then this house sat in the middle of a 960 acre farm, mostly dry land, only one irrigation well. He and a hired man worked hard keeping everything running and doing the planting and harvesting and so forth. It was his bad luck to only have two daughters, no sons.

This was back before Roundup and no-till farming. Weeds had to be hoed by hand. The two of us were Daddy's hoehands—our bad luck. Thank goodness he didn't grow cotton or we'd have also had to pick it, and that would have meant being absent from school. No way Momma would have stood up to him on that score. To say I was unmotivated would have been putting it mildly. I hated being out in the sun and manual labor didn't suit my style. Reading movie magazines like Momma was right up my alley, though.

There we were, hoeing our way down row after row of grain sorghum, me on one row, Margaret across on the one next to me. Never missing a stroke with her own hoe, she looked at me from under her bonnet—Momma made us wear those every day. Margaret said, "If you believe you're fooling anyone into thinking you're working, you're wrong. Daddy'll have you back out here doing it right if you have to work in the dark."

"I'd rather work in the dark. At least I wouldn't have to wear this bonnet."

With the authority she seemed to own, Margaret said, "Going without supper might not suit you, though."

"He wouldn't do that to me."

"Did to me the one and only time I tried slacking off."

"Huh unh."

"Did so. I was eight. That was before you were big enough to use the hoe. He sat at the end of the row and watched till I got every row done right." Just then, she chopped down a careless weed that looked like a redwood. Did it with one strong stroke of her hoe. It was as if each weed posed a personal challenge she was determined to beat. As far as I could see she'd already won. "It was close to midnight when he said I could quit, and I didn't get anything to eat until breakfast the next morning."

"What did Momma say?"

"Like always, not a word. She was happy I was out of the way."

Even young as I was, it didn't surprise me she said that. Later on, I understood the only person Momma ever took up for was herself. We might as well have been strangers just staying at her house, or hired hands.

It galled me to, but I got in gear and cleared my rows as neatly as hers until we finished close to dark. That was the day I knew I would leave this farm as soon as I got out of school. And I wouldn't come back. Any job I had wasn't going to involve farming, and certainly not hoeing. And at ten years old, I promised myself I wouldn't marry a man who farmed, or if I did, he'd have to promise not to make any daughters hoe weeds.

Reminiscing wasn't going to get me any closer to finishing this job, even if Daddy wasn't watching. I pushed the unused underwear to one side, thinking I'd take those and anything else I found that was new to the women's shelter near my apartment in Canyon. That motion uncovered the thing that set me off the worst. A plastic bag holding a batch of Walgreens prescription pill bottles lay under a white cotton nightgown. "Why does this not surprise me? Margaret, why fill those if you didn't intend to take the medicine?"

I tied the twelve bottles (yes, I counted) back into the plastic bag and dropped it on the bed. A year's worth of blood pressure medicine, not a pill missing. I'd doubted the doctor when she told me a preventable stroke killed Margaret. Said it as if my sister had intended to drop dead in the bathroom in the middle of the night. I hadn't argued with the doctor, but that day I hadn't been able to stop my hands from shaking.

Now, seeing those pills, thinking of Margaret choosing to gamble with her life did something to my good sense. I tore the bag open and threw the bottles, one at a time, hard as I could, against the wall. When they'd all landed on the floor, I gathered them up and flung them down again, by twos and threes. The clatter of plastic against hardwood echoed, but too briefly to suit me. And because a safety top never opens when you want it to, I stomped on each one until the floor was dotted with small white and pink pills. That fit left me shaking all over and as dry-eyed as I'd been at the memorial service for her. It took me more than twenty-five miles, until I was nearly back to Canyon, to settle down. I left her ashes in the car when I went inside my apartment.

Every shred of self-control I could summon was required to keep from stalking out of my classroom the next day, and slamming the door. The fifth graders weren't any rowdier than usual, but I woke up intolerant that morning and didn't improve. Finally, I fled as soon as dismissal bell sounded. I had intended not to go out to the home place to finish until I got over being upset. Then I remembered the damn livestock— Margaret's miniature donkey, Cisco, and a flock of guineas. Those birds could fend for themselves and not starve. But Cisco was another matter.

"What use did you have for that donkey? And all the trouble you went to, fencing a corral for him. He's probably been stir-crazy for years, with only this one acre. If you wanted company, the sensible thing to do would have been to get a cat." I paused, as if I were half of a civil conversation. After turning south out of Hereford, crossing the railroad track, I leaned to my right and nudged the urn away from the edge of the passenger seat. "Get back before you fall off. You hate a mess as much as I do." Then after a pause, I said, "Or you could have moved to town and made some real friends."

Watching Cisco munch the hay I put out, and waiting while several of the guineas picked at the feed I'd strewn on the ground, I remembered the time our relatives from East Texas, Momma's kin, came to visit. They'd brought some young guineas as a gift, said they needed no care at all and tasted just like chicken. "All you need to do is learn to catch one when you're hungry," Granddad said. Momma didn't crack a smile. Not out of the ordinary. She seldom did.

After we were in bed that night, Margaret said, "Those little ones are called guinea keets." I wondered how she knew that. And it made me know that our East Texas uncle had been correct. When Momma pushed us toward him to say hello for the first time, he'd said to Margaret, "So you're the smart one." I remembered wondering which one I was.

Later on when some of our daddy's people visited, I heard other relatives talking. One of them said to another, "Too bad for Charlie, wife's too delicate to do much more than cook, and no boys, just girls, one smart and one pretty. He'll likely work hisself into an early grave, what with all this land."

The dresser gaped at me, a dark maw formed by the space left by the drawer I hadn't replaced, leaving in a snit as I had the day before. Now I took my time putting it back and getting the bottom one onto the bed.

Looking at the Timex watch I found in that drawer among other odds and ends, I came to a halt, sitting still on the bed, thinking. Funny thing about the smart versus pretty difference was that as we got older, it worked out more the opposite. She'd finished high school, best in her class, but then didn't take the scholarship that Rice University offered her. Instead of packing up to go to Houston and do something important, she took a one-year vocational nurse program close to home. I was the one who left for college.

Momma got sick and begged her not to leave, to stay and take care of her. Then after she died that next year, Daddy lost his will, just couldn't do a thing but mourn. The next thing lost would be the farm, if someone didn't work it. So Margaret took up doing farm work.

The donkey brayed that funny pipsqueak sound he makes, his intruder alarm. I looked out the window, but no one was there except Cisco staring toward the house. I put the Timex on my wrist. It ran and the sweep second hand still worked.

"Margaret, when you were hiding those pills, telling yourself you'd live forever, did you ever give a thought to who'd take care of Cisco if you just happened to be wrong? He can't live in an apartment with me, and he's too contrary to be in a petting zoo."

I knew she wasn't going to answer, so I wrote myself a reminder to post something on the Hereford community bulletin board on the Internet. Something like—miniature donkey free to good home. "Yes, Margaret, I know, I don't have to live in an apartment and teach school. It was my choice to go to college and have a career. Even if you were the smart one."

I still had four more rooms to go, and standing around talking to myself wouldn't get those cleared out, and then they still had to be cleaned. "No telling how long since you cleaned."

While I waited for the ambulance the day I found her dead, something had made me have the good sense to empty the refrigerator, throw every single thing—milk, eggs, pickles, dried-up cheese, liverwurst, and the half-loaf of white bread off the top—into the trash. But nothing else in the kitchen had been touched. I opened the pantry, aiming to box everything up and give it to some charity. The sight of its shelves jammed with cereal boxes and off-brand vegetables made me just want to sit down.

The urgency that felt like an engine roaring in my chest those first few days after I found Margaret slowed just then to an idling rate, more like a hum than a roar. That sound was all I could hear or think about sitting there. Minutes passed, wasted. The Timex showed eight o'clock and implied I might as well decide—stay the night here or go back to my place and return tomorrow.

"You're right Margaret. Why wouldn't I stay? You left this place to me. An old house and all the responsibility that goes along with it. Plus all that cereal. Thanks."

I stayed. Before I went to bed that night, I'd had supper out of the pantry and cleared out most of the rest. My meal of a can of tuna, a can of tomato soup, and crackers satisfied me better than I expected. For dessert I mixed Cap'n Crunch and some cashews from a never before opened can with some Jif peanut butter.

The next morning, fortified with coffee, peanut butter, and crackers, I switched rooms and started clearing the cabinets and drawers in the bathroom. By noon, I'd managed to fill a trash bag with remainders of typical bathroom supplies, the evidence of intentions for good grooming, some small injuries, and some things for which an explanation didn't come immediately to mind—for example, a box of unused Young Again Six-Week Hair Color- Raucous Red. Besides those things, a lot of items stuck under the sink, at the back, had obviously been there since Daddy died more than twenty-five years ago—a box of Epsom salts gone solid; a near-empty bottle of Sloan's Liniment; a shaving mug, the bristles of its brush slanted sideways from use; and not a trace of anything of Momma's. For that matter, except for that garter belt and panties, not much I found in the house so far would suggest a woman ever lived there. No jewelry box, no cosmetics. The unisex scrub suits and tennis shoes for work and Levi's and tee shirts for home could have belonged to any medium-sized person.

About to quit for the day and go back to my apartment, I wandered into the other bedroom. The twin beds our parents slept in still occupied their same positions on two adjacent sides of the room, each hugging a separate wall. The dresser with the round mirror that had been the only other furniture in that room was no longer there. In its place, Margaret had added a secretarial chair and a desk where a laptop sat alongside a modem and printer. Now that was a surprise.

I lifted the laptop's lid and waited for it to boot up. Maybe she'd been writing poetry. I would like to find that. But truthfully, I expected nothing much to pop up. Since the folks died—actually even before—Margaret and I had lived our lives at a distance. At least that's how it seemed to me. The actual miles weren't many, just enough to give each of us room to be separate people, not as firmly attached as we had been until I went away to school. By then, Margaret had ended up working weekends as a nurse and farming the rest of the time, watching Daddy die by inches.

I know now that I stayed busy with things I could make seem important to fill in part of that space between us. But dammit, one day she'd been showing me how to make it through being a teenager and the next, I was on my own to figure out the rest of it. All my life, I'd been able to see her face, encouraging, guiding me. Then one day and from then on, all I could see was a distant profile.

Well, wouldn't you just know, the computer required a password. It sat there blinking dumbly and inviting me to figure out my sister's mind. The obvious things, various combinations of her birthday, her childhood nickname (Bootsie), and our parents' anniversary got me nothing but frustration. Turning the machine so it faced the wall, I opened the desk drawers, one after another. No password to be found. Although I did turn up a soon-due bill for house insurance. I set that aside, one more thing for me to take care of.

"Inconsiderate, that's what it is. You had to know I'd be the one left to do all this. A considerate person would have at least left some notes. Damned inconsiderate."

Irritated as I was, I couldn't seem to quit. Surely if I tried hard enough, I could figure out the password. Maybe something connected to her work. I'd learned at the memorial service that her work and the people there meant a lot to her, more than I'd expected.

Thinking it was the right thing to do, I'd scheduled a memorial service at the funeral home, and put the date and time (last Saturday, three p.m.) in the local paper. I had fully expected to sit alone with the urn, hymn playing overhead, for the scheduled hour. A person with one relative and no friends isn't likely to draw a crowd.

The recording of "Amazing Grace" began ten minutes before the hour. As if that were a signal, whispered conversation told me someone had joined me and Margaret. Next thing I knew, two women in scrubs filled seats near me on the front row of folding chairs. Before the funeral director led a prayer to begin the service, I counted fourteen people who I guessed were all from the nursing home where she worked. Thank goodness, I'd prepared a eulogy. It was brief. It had to be. There was no way I could say what I really thought.

When the funeral director asked if anyone present wished to share, the response floored me. One of the women, who mentioned she was a nursing assistant who worked with Margaret said, "She was the kindest, most understanding person I ever worked with."

Another stood and said, "Her encouragement and tutoring got me through my nursing courses. Then later, she helped me get the good job I have now in home health."

Several of the others told anecdotes—Margaret working extra shifts when they were short of staff, her keeping others' spirits up by joking when the workload seemed overwhelming, my sister functioning as a role model for new personnel. Not a one of them mentioned her not having the good sense to take care of herself. And none of them spoke of her as a friend, but rather as someone they admired, most likely from a distance. I understood. Without any remaining family members, my own funeral service, if one were even held for me, it would likely be much the same. I knew several people who'd described me in the same terms. A careful listener would hear that I was missed, not loved. No one invites me to happy hour, and if someone did, I'm sure I'd make an excuse.

After the final hymn, each person stopped by to greet me, and one provided the answer to a question that had bothered me. She said, "I was so glad your sister had trusted me with your phone number. She'd said it was in case of emergency. When she didn't come to work or call, I knew something had to be wrong. That's why I called for you right away."

That password had to be somewhere in the house. I tried putting myself in Margaret's place, thinking where I'd hide it, how I'd find it if I forgot. Two minutes later, it came to me. The Bible. Daddy always kept some money stuck in the pages of the big King James Version, for an emergency. Sure enough, there, on the shelf of the end table in the living room lay that big book. I could see my sister giving me that right-eyebrow-raised look she used on me when we were kids as she hand-printed COMPUTER PASSWORD Cisco1994 on that piece of paper I found in front of the first page of Revelation. It worked.

The next morning, Cisco's sound greeted me before I got out of bed. He must have known I stayed to figure out how to get him fed until he could be adopted. Eventually, I found a larger trough in the barn. Putting out two days' of food out at a time would work. The small stock tank for water had a float that kept it full. It wouldn't hurt me to come over and feed him in the afternoons twice a week, and then I could stay here on the weekends. School would be out for the summer in three weeks. "Satisfied Margaret? Don't think I've forgiven you. I just can't stand to see an animal go hungry."

Cisco stood near me, watching as I checked the float. He nosed at my hand, even though he'd just eaten. I patted him and rubbed his ears. He leaned against me. Donkeys must need love, too. Maybe he wants a mate.

In the house, waiting for the computer to start, I wondered when I'd begun thinking of Margaret as a person who wouldn't have a computer. Even though it didn't actually get much use, mine at home had plenty of memory and a fast hard drive, according to the salesperson. But my sister and I were different. My career requires that I stay up to date. I need to follow the news, to network with colleagues, things like that. And her work, well, she never said.

Another surprise confronted me when the computer's desktop revealed itself. An array of apps suggested Margaret had used the machine, and according to the browser's history, she'd used it a lot, regularly. The email inbox showed fifty-three unopened messages. Three dating websites for rural singles— one in Australia, one in the UK, and a third in the USA, each greeted me with a request for an email address and password. More secrets. There'd only been one in the Bible. So I tried it on the first site. No good. Ditto for the other two. "Dammit, Margaret. You don't make anything easy. Why would a person thoughtless enough to gamble with her life bother hiding passwords?"

Don't ask me why I even bothered with the computer and its secrets. I had better things to do. At this rate, I was never going to get this place cleaned out so I could sell it. But I sat right there at that machine for a solid two hours. At first I scouted around more for passwords filed in the machine somewhere. But when I opened the email, I went off on a whole different trail. A separate file, under the inbox, named Ray Kent, held emails as far back as two years. I didn't go further, didn't open any of them. It seemed wrong, reading someone else's private mail.

Besides that one batch in a separate file, each day since Margaret's death, an email had arrived in the inbox from RKB123@gotomail.com, Ray Kent, I was pretty sure. "Well, Margaret. There's yet another thing for me to clean up. Had you told this person you were slowly committing suicide and not to be surprised if one day you didn't answer? What do you want me to do? I'm tempted to ignore these letters, just the way you ignored your blood pressure."

I shut down the computer and left the room. Then I locked the house and drove, first to Hereford where I ate a Dude and a Blizzard from the Dairy Queen. I never eat fast food. From there I drove directly to my apartment. Now I can't recall anything about the rest of that day.

It was midweek before I went out there again, and I stayed only long enough to put out feed for the donkey and the birds. Margaret kept me awake until after midnight every night that week and fatigue left me with barely enough tolerance to get through the end-of-year faculty meeting on Friday. After the meeting, the principal stopped me and said, "Is there something you and I need to talk about?"

"Not that I know of."

"Nothing at all? I haven't received your signed contract for next year, so I wondered."

"Slipped my mind." I glanced at the Timex. "Sorry, I need to go. Animals to feed."

I didn't look back as I left.

Actually, it wasn't my sister who disrupted my sleep, but it was the two of us together. Those hours in the dark were filled with replays of conversations we had over the years. With those exchanges laid end-to-end that way, like a "greatest hits retrospective marathon," it was possible to see us grow alike, then separate, then distant. The final scene in which the content was substantial happened nearly twenty years ago, when Daddy died and we sold the land. Farming had become too much for her, she'd admitted. Bad as she hated to let it go, it was best. "I can't do it alone, and I can't afford to hire help," she'd said.

My brisk reply, delivered in my full of authority, elementary teacher voice was, "If you can't, you can't. Selling is the only rational course of action."

Margaret let a sigh escape. She said, "I'll take care of it. When it sells, you'll get half."

"I can always use the money. Invest it for my retirement."

Someone should have slapped me.

The reruns stopped then. I couldn't see Margaret's face anymore. I imagined her replaced by a flickering light, as when the final frames run out of a projector.

As I drove toward the home place that afternoon, I wondered what Margaret had done with her half. My $95,000 had been earning for all those years, working the magic of compound interest to come now to about $220,000. Margaret was named the "pay on death" owner of that account that is my nest egg. I'd assumed her accounts were set up the same, since it was only the two of us. That was something else we'd never discussed. The rest of our conversations had been by phone, a ritual conducted the first Sunday of each month. She always called at eleven and opened with, "Have time to talk? I don't want to make you late for the sermon."

We'd both laugh and then, soon after, I'd say, "I'm glad everything's okay with you. Thanks for calling. Bye."

Cisco didn't make a sound when I drove up. He trotted to me and nuzzled my hand even before I fed him. The guineas scurried around my feet in a welcoming, hopeful gray mass. The rest of the weekend, I'd intended to finish clearing and start cleaning, but exhaustion made sleep and brushing and petting Cisco my only accomplishments.

The last two weeks of school trudged by. As usual, the final day was filled with a track and field meet, an assembly, book return, locker cleanout, and other necessary, anticlimactic activity. The principal usually held an informal post-dismissal reception for teachers, everyone assembled in the lounge. I had planned a quick exit through the side door.

At the home place that afternoon, after taking care of Cisco and the birds, I took in the first load of my clothes I'd packed. Next came the food from my apartment. I planned to stay a week or two. I would get the rest of the housework done, tend to legal and financial matters, find a home for Cisco, and eliminate Margaret's presence from the digital world. After four trips in and out, I had unloaded everything from the car except for the urn. As I carried it in, I said, "You have no right to complain. I've had a lot to do, and all of it's your fault."

Sleeping late would have been a deserved treat, but the hum threatened to become a roar again. Things needed doing. So the next morning at 6:30, after a single cup of coffee, I switched on the vacuum cleaner. By nine the bedroom's condition satisfied me. Blinds and baseboards dusted, closet cleared except for the things I'd brought. I moved on to the living room and vacuumed there. Whoever bought the place would surely want to replace the room's 1980s sculptured shag. Until then, I'd keep it clean.

Stopping only to eat, I continued cleaning, and finished the living room and started on the second bedroom. But when I looked at the urn sitting on the desk, I knew I had to gather some information. The cemetery was near the south edge of town, "easy to get to," people had always said. For years I didn't realize that was an attempt at a joke. Margaret once said I didn't have much of a sense of humor. As I drove to the cemetery, I tried to convince myself I did, but not a single laughable thing came to mind.

Margaret knew better than to fault my memory, though. Sure enough, I'd been correct when I thought that Daddy and Momma's graves were the only two in the family plot. No other spaces remained. I suppose they expected we'd both get married and be buried with our own families. We didn't.

Back at the house I spoke to Margaret again—she in the urn in the bedroom that I now called her office, me in the kitchen. "If you had any preference about your ashes, you never told me. So if it matters to you now, you'd better tell me. Otherwise it's either sit where you are from now on, or I'll walk outside and open the lid and let the West Texas wind take care of you."

I waited a few seconds, then went to her office. If a person were to put a bookcase in place of one of those beds and a day bed in place of the other, that room could be very useful. "You had your chance. I've decided you're staying here with me, like it or not."

I switched on the computer and as soon as it came to life, I opened the email. Pushing aside my scruples about reading others' mail, I opened the one that had come that morning from RKB123.

Dear Margaret,

Please let me know how you are and if I have done something to offend you. It's not like you to not reply, so I am terribly concerned.

I sat with my fingers hovering over the keys. The only way to know if I should reply was to read their correspondence, to see if he mattered to Margaret. As soon as I thought it, I told myself that was an elaborate rationalization born of my nosiness. What they'd written was none of my business. I didn't have to know what they'd shared or what they might have planned before I could tell him she had died.

The hum I felt in my whole body accelerated, threatened to rise to its previous roar.

I hoped they had been in love, that my sister had let herself find closeness with a man in a way I never really had, that I might never be capable of. But if she had, and hadn't told me, I couldn't bear knowing it. We'd been close. A long time ago.

I opened the UK rural singles website. For a password, I inserted EDIE, her childhood nickname for me. I could imagine her smiling as she chose it. Promptly, the site welcomed Margaret back. With a few keystrokes, I selected "no longer seeking" from the list of reasons one might give for deleting a profile. An automated reply mentioned I would receive an evaluation form and congratulated me for finding someone compatible. As if they knew.

After that, with a few mouse clicks the other two sites also released my sister. I avoided thinking about what they would do with the evidence of her identity. I'd read about data mining.

The hum continued, but at a lower pitch.

The next morning, as soon as I woke the computer, a tone notified me of an incoming email. It was from RKB. I opened it as if it were mine.

Dear Margaret, Over these past two years I have come to rely on our being in touch each day, either by email or phone. It's been over a month.

The sudden loss of our connection takes away some of each day's luster. I wish now I had tried harder to overcome your objections to our meeting in person. I would have made the trip, regardless of distance. Not knowing where you are and not hearing from you make me fear the worst. Please write or call.

Yours,

Ray Kent Bailey

At least I knew Margaret was gone for good. And I knew why. This man didn't know. But Ray Kent Bailey could be a fictitious name, some scammer in a foreign country trying to retrieve a mark who strayed. The simplest thing to do would be to close Margaret's email account and call it done. I didn't owe an explanation to anyone.

If intention were measured in inches, I was about one inch away from closing the account when Cisco brayed. It wasn't his usual demand for food, but a frantic, higher pitched call I hadn't heard before. I sighted him out the window. He stood alone in the corral facing the house—no sign of any intruder.

I returned to the keyboard and opened the file labeled Ray Kent. I read each of the emails, beginning with the first one two years ago. They had met on the US rural singles site. Both had provided vague information about location; Margaret listed "rural West Texas" and his profile had said "rural New Mexico." Those might as well have said "somewhere in a 250,000 square mile space west of I 35 and south of Oklahoma and Colorado." Both of them were cautious, it appeared. At first, they exchanged notes about once a week. Then once daily, then twice daily, without fail. Reading through the file, I watched as a friendship developed, then bloomed.

They spoke of the weather; their work—his as foreman on a ranch thirty miles outside Las Vegas, New Mexico, Margaret factually describing hers as chief nurse in a long-term care facility; their ages—born the same year, 1949; hobbies— both readers and neither enjoyed television; pets—he has a house dog named Skip and a working cow dog named Taffy and Margaret spoke of Cisco as good company. He attached a photograph of himself and the two dogs. His eyes said he was a kind man. She replied with a picture of her with Cisco, a sort of out of focus selfie.

It was only after nine months that they shared telephone numbers, at his request, and then only after promising one another never to call unless there was an emergency or an "appointment" for a call.

I saw them begin telling stories from their pasts and sharing details of their family histories. Margaret described me as a highly accomplished teacher who had encouraged many younger teachers by serving as mentor during their practice teaching. "I'm proud of her for all she's done," her note said. They both spoke of never having married and offered no further details on that topic. Then about a year ago, he asked if they could meet—he had a week of vacation coming and no plans. Margaret replied she had to be on call every night. He told her the actual miles between them (only 231, he said) and offered to meet in Clovis, New Mexico. She'd only be fifty miles from her work.

As if I were reading a novel, I urged the characters to quit being so careful, to take a chance on finding some happiness with another human being. In her next email, she declined firmly. She had signed it "Fondly, Margaret." The reply he sent sounded understanding.

I pushed back from the desk and looked toward the urn sitting on the bookshelf. I said, "Oh Margaret, why didn't you tell me? Why not take the chance?"

I knew what her answer would have been—she hadn't for the same reason I never let myself choose love or even real friendship—for no reason that either of us could name.

I couldn't stop the tears that began falling. The hum in my chest stopped the minute I allowed the sorrow for my sister, for her and Ray Kent, and for myself to pour out. After a while, when I could breathe regularly, I began an email to Ray Kent Bailey. I got as far as Dear Mr. Bailey, and couldn't continue.

Leaving the machine open, cursor blinking, I went out to Cisco's pen and began the work I'd thought about earlier. With winter coming sooner than I'd like, that little creature would need more protection from the weather than the stack of hay bales Margaret had piled against the north wall of the barn. A couple of hours later, I had hung the garden tools on pegs, cleared out trash accumulated in corner, and marked off a space about eight feet square in the southeast corner. Tomorrow I'd find a carpenter to build the two additional sides that would make a stall in that space. Cisco watched me as I worked and stood near when I stopped to rest. When I went back to the computer, the words for Ray Kent came more easily.

I am Margaret's sister, Edith. I am sorry I have to give you this news in such an impersonal way. Margaret died the day of the last email she sent to you. Her death was sudden and unexpected, a stroke.

In the process of taking care of her unfinished business, I came across your correspondence here. Please forgive my having read the letters between you two. I did so out of caution, and reading them convinced me that you are the person you represented yourself to be. It is clear that your friendship was important to Margaret. Thank you for being a good friend.

Sincerely, Edith Barlow

That evening I read and reread his reply. In a bare, direct way that surprised me, he told me how much their friendship had meant to him. Then at the end of his note, he asked if I would mind if he wrote to me again. It said, *I think we are both alone now and sadder for this loss. We have that in common.*

Weeks later, when July twentieth arrived, it brought a call from the principal at my school. I let it go to voice mail. I stopped brushing Cisco and played the message. Her voice sounded as if she were thousands of miles away. "Hi, Edith, I'm sorry to have missed you. It's important that you and I talk. I need your signed contract to confirm your position for the next school year. Summer is flying by and planning is underway. Please call when you receive this message."

Cisco brayed at the sound of a train whistle in the distance, and leaned against me as he waited. That grooming has become our daily ritual since I moved to the home place. I closed the phone, and ran the brush across his left side in three long strokes. Then I patted him on the rump. "You look handsome enough. I'm going in; I've got something to do now."

My letter of resignation had sat as a draft for several weeks. I printed it and found a stamp. I let Cisco out of the corral. He trotted beside me as I walked to the mailbox at the end of the driveway.

Missing

"If you're a burglar, please come in the front door so I don't have to get out of my chair!" Fern yelled that as soon as she heard Kellen at the back door. The cleaning woman had just left through the front, so it was safe to joke a little. Maybe Kellen would even smile.

Nothing had seemed normal since the theft. Kellen had said as soon as she walked in that Sunday three weeks back to catch up, she knew that something wasn't right. Fern didn't doubt it. Some people are like that, extra perceptive. Kellen was one of them. That was part of what made people in town say they'd sooner have her for their doctor than a doctor. Not that Kellen ever pretended. She knew just how far her nurse practitioner education went and made sure the patients did, too. Her back-up doctor over in Plainview was as close as a phone call.

Until all this mess, coming to work at the clinic had been the biggest joy of Fern's life. Kellen depended on her. More than once she'd said the clinic couldn't run if Fern wasn't there. Just the two of them—Kellen taking care of patients and Fern doing everything else. Except the cleaning. Thank goodness there was money in their budget for the woman who came in after hours to keep things spotless. Fern had spent a lot of time finding the right person, someone who knew how a bathroom ought to look and smell and who knew without being told that baseboards had to be dusted at least once a week.

But that theft and the nurse practitioner Kellen had hired two weeks earlier leaving without notice, and apparently being involved with the thief, had turned Kellen grim. Fern couldn't help feeling sad for her. They'd caught the guy who actually stole the drugs and money within a few days. But the nurse hadn't been found the last time the sheriff stopped in. Maybe today he'd bring some good news. So far, he'd been tight-lipped every time he turned up. He was the only one who kept his mouth shut. Seemed like everyone in town had an opinion about what happened and who did it, and they shared those opinions freely. Fern had gotten good at telling people there was nothing to tell.

Kellen sat down in the chair next to Fern's behind the front reception counter. She dropped her bag on the floor. "I'm going to decide which one of those computerized record systems to buy. And soon. Carrying these charts home to review convinced me." She pointed to her bag, which fell on its side. Two charts slid out onto the floor. "That batch must weigh twenty pounds. I reviewed them all. Everything's up to date."

"That's a good thing, isn't it?" Fern gave up on smiling. Kellen looked like she hadn't eaten in days—her face drawn, pale except for the blue shadows under her eyes. "I brought us a couple of those burritos you like. They're on your desk." She'd also made chocolate chip cookies. Kellen never refused one of those.

"Thanks. I forgot breakfast. Everyone at the house moved in slow motion this morning."

She emptied the charts from her bag, stacked them on the desk. "When you have time, these can be filed. I'll be in the back."

"First patient's not till nine. Why don't you go ahead and eat?"

She watched Kellen walk toward Exam Room 1, moving like she was wading upstream against rushing water. Something else must be wrong. It could be one of her children. Surely it wasn't trouble with her husband. But Kellen kept a lot to herself. Fern understood.

Nancy Reese, always heavy but even more so in the last year, pushed open the front door. A gust chased a measure of dust in as she struggled to get through the door. When she finally did, she stopped and fussed with her hair, then said, "Wind's already up; I'd say we're in for a blow today."

From where she sat, Fern could see Nancy didn't have to worry about finding an anchor if it did. They'd been to high school together. Along with Kellen's mother, Nancy had been one of Fern's friends. Maybe that was using the term loosely; they'd spent quite a bit of time together. Even before she married Junior, Nancy was one to look down her nose at people. Fern always wondered what made her think she had the right. Her people didn't move to town until she was in eighth grade, so it wasn't as if they were old money or, for that matter, any money. Her dad had worked at Proctor's filling station as a mechanic.

"How've you been, Nancy? I haven't seen you in town in a while."

"I've been at our vacation house in New Mexico all summer, Red River. Junior got over when he could."

Fern gave her a nod, trying to hint she believed it. She knew Junior hadn't missed many days at the coffee shop down the street. "Have a good time?"

"Just great." She leaned against the counter, directly in front of Fern. "I loved every minute." Her voice trailed off on the last two words, close to a whisper.

Fern rolled her chair back a few inches, looked up at Nancy. "Mmmm. You here for a follow up this morning or something new?" She didn't expect an answer. She only asked so she could see Nancy's face. That stricken expression—the silent movie virgin in peril—always made Fern's mouth twitch, hiding a laugh.

"Pain in my limbs. Excruciating."

"Kellen'll be with you in just a few minutes. Till then, you probably ought to sit down, get off your feet."

Fern ducked her head, looking at a stain on her desk, until the urge to roll her eyes passed. Maybe Nancy really was sick. She hadn't even asked about the burglary. Fern abandoned studying the desktop and said, "Can I bring you a glass of water or something while you wait?"

By noon, Kellen had taken care of seven patients and Fern had filled all eight afternoon appointment spaces. It amazed her how Kellen convinced every person who walked in they were her one and only concern. Always brought them to the front when they left, the way you would a departing guest. Fern knew her well enough to tell she was running on fumes.

Fern locked the front door just after twelve. "I brought lunch enough for both of us. Let's sit and not talk at all for a few minutes, just eat."

She heard Kellen's sigh all the way across the waiting room. "Do I look that bad, Fern?"

"I brought tuna sandwiches and carrots. Healthy food. Energy food." Truth was, it wasn't just that Kellen looked like a ghost; bringing lunch helped Fern as much as it did Kellen. Looking for all kinds of busy work kept her from dwelling on her own troubles.

Another sigh, then Kellen walked to her office. Fern followed, lunch bags in hand, shaking her head at the sight of Kellen's slumped shoulders. "And don't forget we have cookies, too."

She spread the food on the desk and sat in the chair facing Kellen's. "I know I promised not to talk, but I just need to ask. Is something else going on besides the theft and Sandra quitting, almost before she got started?"

Kellen shook her head, then picked up a half sandwich and took a bite, chewed for a long time. Fern held her breath, waiting for her to swallow. She said, "I'll get us something to drink. Milk, Diet Coke, water?"

When Fern returned from the break room with a bottle of water and a carton of milk, she said, "If there is, you know you can tell me. It won't go anywhere."

Kellen nodded. After one more bite of the sandwich she rewrapped it in the foil and zipped it into the plastic bag. Fern edged the bag of cookies across the desk toward Kellen's right hand. "Fresh. Made 'em last night."

Again, the nod. Fern had to give it to her, anyone who didn't know, people who didn't see her this way, would think everything was just dandy. The girl could gut it up when she needed to.

Fern knew about pasting on a happy face and getting on with things. All year long, since her daughter left town last New Year's day, she'd been doing everything she could short of calling the law to try to find her. Meanwhile, she'd worked her hardest not to let on to anyone. Some days that was easier said than done.

Her husband had always been the one the girl favored. So when she left, Fern spent a lot of time thinking he knew where she'd gone. Finally, one night at supper sometime around the middle of January, she said, "I've been thinking a lot about where Wendy would have gone. She wouldn't have left without someplace to go."

He looked up from his meatloaf and potatoes and said, "That makes sense."

"And she wouldn't have left without plenty of money. She never touched that little savings account. I checked." She waited until he looked up from his plate. "Tell me the truth. Did you give her money at Christmas you didn't tell me about?"

He swore he didn't. "Look, I don't know a bit more than you do about where she is. If you don't think she's going to come back on her own, when she's good and ready, we could get the law on it, but you know as well as I do, if they bring her back, she'll leave again," he said.

She pushed back her plate. "I don't believe you. More than once I told her no when she wanted something and you gave her money, like that phone she wanted back in high school."

"That was a long time ago. Over and done." He polished off the mashed potatoes.

Without leaving her chair, she stacked their two plates and moved the rest of the dishes into a crowd at the edge of the table. "She always knew she could get what she wanted from you. Made out that I never understood her. She had no idea how much I wanted everything right for her. No idea."

If she hadn't been so close to tears, she'd have kept on saying everything that had stacked up in her since Wendy had left. The silverware in her right hand threatened to clatter to the floor. She let it drop into the empty potato bowl.

He said, "Blaming me isn't going to make her come back." He left that hanging there, and pushed back his chair. "If you want to call the sheriff, go ahead. I won't interfere. But it's a waste of time. Won't accomplish anything but make you, us, more miserable."

In the end, Fern agreed because she knew he was probably right, but she hadn't liked it. She went to bed with dirty dishes on the table.

Since then, except that note Wendy left behind saying she had to learn to be on her own, nothing gave them a clue. That and one phone call back in July offering only, "I'm fine. Don't worry about me."

But not a day went by that Fern didn't ask herself why, what she'd done that made Wendy leave.

Kellen stood and looked out the window. Without turning around, she said, "I blame myself. This might have been prevented."

Fern said, "I'll put that sandwich in the refrigerator. Maybe you'll want it later." She cleared the food away, replaced everything except the cookies in one of the brown paper lunch bags.

She knew that at twenty-three, her daughter probably should be on her own. They'd babied her all her life. They'd about given up; how many thirty-six year-old women get pregnant after trying for seventeen years? The girl had every reason to be rotten.

But until she took up with that cowboy from one of those ranches over the state line in New Mexico, Wendy never gave them a minute's trouble. Dated a few boys in high school, nothing serious. Had lots of girl friends, most of them married and left town by now. She commuted to junior college, and right after she graduated, took a job as a teacher's aide at the elementary. Then she just up and left in the night.

Fern returned to Kellen's office, and sat down again. She watched Kellen until she turned from the window. After a long silence, Kellen said, "I could make a thousand excuses about the theft, but nothing justifies what I didn't do."

Kellen crumpled into her chair again, leaned back, and closed her eyes. After too short a rest, she sat forward, pulled a cookie out of the bag, and bit into it. "Maybe they were right. I don't know how to run this or anything else."

"Who?"

"Everybody who expected this clinic to fail. Me to fail."

"Anyone in particular?"

"My mother, for one."

"Want another cookie for later? I'm going to make a bathroom stop before the afternoon starts."

Kellen took a cookie, placed it on the desk pad. "I'm sorry to whine. You're kind to listen to me." She ran her fingers through her hair. "Do I need lipstick?"

"You're kind of pale."

"Shows, huh?"

Fern nodded, then drew a deep breath. "It's not my place to say this, but I will. I know you're wrong about your mother. She's proud of you. Always has been."

Kellen was standing at the window again, staring out. Fern wondered if all mothers and daughters misunderstood each other, and ended up at odds until it was too late.

In the bathroom, looking at herself in the mirror, Fern teased her hair up a little in the back, wondering again if she ought to color it instead of letting the gray show. Mother had kept hers dark until the day she died. Although she often missed her mother, last January after Wendy left, Fern had been glad she had already passed on. The woman would have been on her like a gnat, like she had been when Fern first got pregnant. Her mother never missed a day all nine months, telling her she was too old to have a baby in the first place. Maybe she'd been right. Fern knew she'd made mistakes with Wendy, plenty of them. But nobody ever tried harder.

She kept busy with patients and insurance claims after lunch until about three when the mailman waltzed in after finishing his rural route. He wagged a handful of envelopes in one hand and a box about twelve inches square under his other arm. He was another one who knew how to convince folks everything was dandy. Always clowning a little, like he had an audience. Never failed to make Fern smile. "I come bearing mail!" he said.

"Aside from drug company ads and the circular from the furniture store, what did you bring?"

"This box looks interesting." If she gave him half a chance, he'd hang around until she opened it.

"Samples, I imagine." She put the envelopes on the desk and the box under the counter. "Thanks. See you tomorrow." She looked over his shoulder at Carlene Lewis coming in the door, toting her two-year-old on her right hip. Seeing that made Fern smile, too. She'd hardly ever let Wendy's feet hit the ground either. Not until she weighed too much to carry, about the time she was four.

"Off on my appointed rounds, spreading cheer all over the county. Till tomorrow!" He delivered his parting line, the same one every day, and added a little salute.

Kellen came from the back and invited Carlene and her daughter, LaTosha, to come with her. She had taken off her white lab coat, like she always did. It seemed to work; hardly any of the kids started screaming as soon as they saw her.

Fern knew it didn't make a bit of sense, but the stack of envelopes gave her a tiny bit of hope. Any mail did. One day there'd be a letter from Wendy. Not here, probably, more likely at home. One by one, she read the address and the return on each of today's items—all to Kellen or to the clinic. Fern's hope seldom vanished entirely in the absence of encouragement; it only receded a bit. There would still be possibilities waiting in the box at home.

The rest of the afternoon patients were in and out and then the waiting room stood empty by four-fifteen. Five minutes later, the sheriff parked out front. Fern watched him put on his hat, glance up in his rearview mirror, and adjust his hat before marching in the front door.

By the time he got to the reception desk, he'd worked up a big smile. "Is Kellen here?" You'd have thought he was Kellen's uncle, not the law from Littlefield. Fern looked him square in the eye. She'd voted for the other candidate in the last election. She said, "Yes, Sheriff, Mrs. Harmon just finished with the last patient of the day. Would you like to speak with her?"

"Yes." Then he added, "Thank you."

Kellen was staring out her office window again when Fern rapped on the doorsill. "Sheriff Clark wants to see you."

"I'll come up there so you can hear what he has to say, too."

Kellen offered the man a chair in the waiting area. He preferred to stand, he said, lots to do. "I wanted to bring you up to date on our progress about the nurse who left so suddenly. We got her name from the fellow we arrested when he decided to plea bargain. Named her as an accomplice. But he denied knowing where to find her. In the past few days, we located and interviewed her mother. She lives down near San Saba, father's dead. Says she hasn't seen her in four years, since the girl finished her Master's degree in Austin. Gets a money order from her in the mail every so often. No letter, no return address. Said she'd tried to find her lots of times. Got to wonder, though." His phone rang, and he pulled it out of his shirt pocket. To Kellen he said, "Sorry, got to take this." He turned away. Fern couldn't hear any of his brief conversation. Next thing she knew, he spoke as he walked toward the door, then turned, holding it open, letting in the dust. "I'll let you know when, or if, we turn her up."

Fern watched him drive away. She said, "You can bet her mother did everything she could to try to find her."

She felt Kellen's hand on her shoulder and then heard her walk away toward her office.

Fern stared out at the parking space vacated by the sheriff. How dare he judge that woman? His attitude was the very reason she'd finally agreed with her husband not to file a missing person report about Wendy. He immediately assumed that the woman in San Saba made mistakes raising Sandra, or that she'd been a bad mother is some other ways, and so the girl didn't want anything to do with her. And that last thing he said showed he doubted she'd tried to find her. He had no idea how much time and money she'd put into finding her. She'd probably even hired a private investigator.

For four months after Wendy disappeared, Fern ratholed money, not telling her husband. Then, the first of May, when she had the three hundred the PI said it would cost up front, she told him. Not asking, just matter of fact, said she was going to hire the man the next day. Her husband had given her a long look and then hugged her. All he said was, "You do what you need to do."

The investigator turned up about three weeks later, saying he'd done "an exhaustive search" and would need more money to continue. Fern had said, "You tell me you haven't found a trace of Wendy. Well, you haven't shown me a trace of what you've done to try, either. I'm not paying any more until I see some result from that first three hundred dollars."

As if he expected the question, the man had pulled two sheets of paper out of his inside jacket pocket. All it was was a print out of an Internet search. It verified Wendy's last known address correctly. Right there at home. That was it. Fern told the man she didn't need his services further. It was two days before she could tell her husband about that without crying.

Still, she didn't give up. Once a week, every week, she called at least three of the girls who were Wendy's friends, one of her teachers at the community college, and the administrative office at the local school, in case they'd had a request for a reference. So far, all that effort only made her feel sad and a little desperate. She'd been close to giving up several times. But today, that sheriff and his attitude made her more convinced than ever that there had to be something she could do to find Wendy.

She told herself she was being hypersensitive. But she couldn't help it. That remark the sheriff made, implying that poor woman in San Saba didn't do all she could nagged at her all week long.

Saturday morning, as soon as she had her coffee, she started all over again with her own Internet detective work. First, she used simple name searches and dutifully followed each link, only to find that each Wendy Barker was someone else's daughter. After the searching with Internet Explorer, Google, and Bing, she haunted Facebook, where she was surprised that morning to find a group called, "I grew up in Sudan, Texas." Lots of people she'd forgotten, who'd moved away, showed up there. Not Wendy.

Moving on, Fern searched LinkedIn, Spokeo, Goodreads, and Classmates. The only result of all that searching was that Fern resolved that whenever Wendy returned, she'd never sign on to any of those places again. What a waste of time. All of it.

The kitchen chair's stiff back reminded her she'd been on the hunt that morning for a long time. She stood, and just then she heard her husband say, from somewhere in another room, "I'm hungry. Want to ride over to Muleshoe and eat Mexican food?"

Before she could answer, he appeared in the doorway to the living room. He said, "At it again?"

She closed the laptop. "I'm in the mood for some enchiladas. That's a good idea." Another argument wasn't going to change anything. No matter what, she would find Wendy, with or without his help. "I'll get my purse if you're ready to go."

He didn't move, just leaned against the door frame like he might stay a while. "Find anything?"

Fern shook her head. "Are we going in your pickup or the car?"

"How long before you admit what's obvious? Wendy doesn't want us to find her."

She took care not to let herself shout. "That's not so. Someone or something's keeping her from it. I know."

"You've spent hours since she left searching on that computer. And then you spent money to get nothing from that detective. That girl is spoiled, and yes, I know it's partly my fault. But she thinks only of herself. Making yourself sick worrying and searching won't bring her back."

Fern drew in a long, deep breath and stared at her husband. "Giving up on her, calling her self-centered won't, for sure. I'm not asking you to put out any effort. Just stay out of my way."

She pushed past him, into the living room. She grabbed her purse off the couch. "If we're going, let's go."

Trailing her as she went out the front door, he said, "We'll take my pickup."

"That's fine with me. I don't need your comments on my driving today."

He hung around the house all day long after they got back. That night, around ten, he left his recliner and went to the front porch to smoke one last cigarette before bed. Fern waited until she heard him head to the bedroom. Then she opened the computer again and went to the people search sites that charged fees. She'd already paid for unlimited access for three months on two sites. Nothing had changed since last week when she checked. About midnight she slipped into bed. He didn't move.

Things rocked along at the clinic, with no further word from the sheriff. Slowly Kellen's vigor returned. Fern could tell by the way she walked. Plus the shadows that marred her pretty face disappeared. Fern wished she'd have been able to be more uplifting during those weeks, but she'd been so worried about Wendy. Every time she heard or read the words "human trafficking," her whole body turned cold. It had been all she could do some days to get to work.

Along with her usual energy, Kellen's appetite returned. That morning, as soon as she came in the back door, she said to Fern, "Don't make lunch plans. I've brought a little celebration for us."

"Little celebration" didn't do justice to the spread Kellen laid out on her desk at noon. After plenty of fried chicken and potato salad and assorted trimmings, she unveiled dessert—chocolate cupcakes with smiling ghosts atop the thick frosting.

She said, "I think we should put up some decorations in the waiting area, to celebrate Fall. I'd like to do witches and goblins, but some these days believe that's bad for children."

Fern said, "Let me. I have lots of decorations at the house. Halloween's always been Wendy's favorite holiday." She took a long time separating the cupcake from the paper baking cup. Without meeting Kellen's eyes, she licked orange frosting off her right index finger. "I'll probably need a nap about two o'clock."

"Maybe we should change our clinic hours. Siesta every day from two until three."

Fern kept her head down, clearing their scraps. She said, "I'm for that." Then she coughed to cover up the way her voice felt choked. She wouldn't spoil that girl's good mood by breaking out in tears.

The day before Halloween, Fern watched as Kellen stood at the clinic's front door, waving goodbye to the day's last patient. She followed as Kellen walked back to her office. She said, "That's the last one. I locked the front. If you have a minute, I need to tell you something before you go." She stood at the door and watched Kellen stuff her stethoscope in her bag. "It won't take long, but I just have to tell you."

Kellen sat and pointed at the other office chair. "Sure. What? Tell it before you burst."

Fern perched on the chair, leaning across the desk. "Oh, honey, I did something I never would have thought I'd do. I went to see a psychic. And you'll never believe what she told me. Did you ever go to a psychic?"

Kellen shook her head. "No, I wouldn't even know where to find one."

"I've just had this strongest feeling lately that I'm going to find Wendy, or that she'll come home. But I thought maybe there was something I was supposed to do, you know, to push things along, let her know we aren't upset, just concerned. I've thought all along maybe . . ." She shrugged. "I don't know what I thought. But then I found this ad."

She waved a bright red card with the words, ALL IS WELL, printed above some other information, then stuck it back in her pocket. "I didn't even tell my husband, I just dialed that number and made an appointment. She's in Lubbock. I know you need to leave, but I just want you to know. Here's what she told me. Wendy is fine and she will come back, not soon, but she will. Meanwhile, I should just think positive thoughts for her."

"What made the psychic believable to you?"

"From the time I walked in, I felt comfortable with her. She was like a regular person, about my age. No crystal ball, no funny clothes. And a real soothing voice."

Kellen hesitated, then said, "Nothing suspicious about her at all?"

"Not a bit. And when we started talking, that woman knew lots of things no one would know if she wasn't, you know, tuned in."

"Did she tell you to come back to see her?"

"No. My husband was sure she was after more money. But no. I paid her fifty dollars and she said again, 'All is well.' And when I left, she told me I could come back any time I wanted to."

"That sounds like a positive message. I can see why you're excited."

"Do you think it's crazy? Do you think there are people who know things before they happen?"

Fern knew the answer. Kellen couldn't possibly doubt, knowing the things the way she does. She would never try to steal her hope.

Then, with a smile that told it all, Kellen said, "Fern, I believe anything is possible. I'm glad she helped you."

Telling Kellen had made her hope seem real and realistic. Fern felt her shoulders relax. No more computer searches. She'd trust Wendy to come back when she was ready. She checked her watch. "You need to leave. I'll go after I clean up the front desk. Thanks for listening."

Kellen said, "Let's both go now." With her bag over her shoulder, she came around her desk. "I'm so glad for you."

As they walked together toward the door, Fern felt a strong, warm hand on her back.

Thirst

The first phase of the mission I'd been assigned required that I get my father dressed in something other than the blue knit outfit he called his jogging clothes and out of the house no later than nine a.m. It wasn't going to be easy. Since he retired from farming he sleeps late. So, on Monday morning, when Dad opened his front door before I even knocked, and he was already dressed in Levi's and a starched shirt and wearing his best Silver Belly Stetson at seven a.m., it threw a wrench in my plan.

My mother had left Sunday on a trip with her sister. I won't bore you with the details of their travel, but the upshot was that several days ago, she'd gotten me to agree to "check on" my dad twice a day for the week she'd be gone. It made no sense to me. L.G. Brackett seldom took kindly to supervision. But the way a good son should, I agreed. Later, I figured out I'd said yes to "checking on your father" way too soon.

Here's exactly the way it went. She said, "I don't just mean check to see if he's breathing. You'll have to be sure he eats. If I'm not here to make his meals, he's likely to starve just to spite me."

Mistaking that as an idea that could be countered with simple logic, I said, "I doubt he'd do without food for a whole week."

I might as well have just nodded. She never slowed down. "You have no idea. He expects three meals a day on the table, just like when he worked the farm. And he expects me to cook them. Then there's the matter of his medicine. All his pills

will be in the correct slots in that pill box on the kitchen bar.
You'll have to see that he takes them."

As far as I knew, Dad didn't take any medicine. He never
went to the doctor, and at eighty-one, has never even been
hospitalized. Unless they'd lied to me all my life. Well, there was
that one time, but I wouldn't call that a real hospitalization.
More like a multipurpose stay in a rest facility. Way back. The
man had been quite the rounder earlier in his life.

"What pills is he taking?"

"They'll all be in the box. Time doesn't matter. Just see
he gets them every day."

After a couple more instructions that let me know she'd
put some effort into making up reasons for me to pay attention
to him for seven days, she launched into a story. It was about
how she'd made an accidental phone call. "I never intended to
call Doris Jean, but then I heard her talking, from my purse. I
hauled my phone out and asked if she needed help. She said I
called her but not to worry, she'd done the same thing, only
worse. She butt dialed the preacher one day. I started to be
scandalized because I didn't know what she meant until she
explained butt dialing. I guess I'll be goofy until the day I die."
We laughed about butt dialing, and I stood up to leave.

She followed me toward the front door, then said, "Oh,
wait. There's one more . . ."

Her voice trailed off when she left the room. I could
hear her talking but couldn't understand. Then she came back
from the direction of their bedroom and said, "I think you're the
only one who can convince him." She handed me a batch of
some sort of brochures. "A week ought to give you time. I don't
really care whether it's Amarillo or Lubbock. Anywhere but here.
Has to have a good dining room. I'm not kidding. I'm through
cooking, for good."

Now before I tell you the rest, you need to know
something I've learned about my mother. Just like a mediocre
gambler or a pathological liar, she has some "tells" that give her
away. And hers aren't something as simple as a twitch of her
eyebrows or clearing her throat. For about the first forty years of

my life, I didn't know. Then my wife explained it to me. This was back when she and I used to sit and talk and have a drink every day when I came in from work.

That evening she'd said, "I have to tell you, I admire your mother." One thing about my wife—she's a very good observer—astute, you might say. Admiring my mother didn't come out of the blue. She was about to pass along something important.

She said, "She knows exactly how to manage you. If a person didn't know her, they wouldn't see how slick she is. First she gets you to agree to do something for her, anything—a small request—pick up something at the grocery store, give her some advice about seeing a doctor, whatever. She makes it clear you're the only person truly qualified to take care of her need, that she is so glad she has you to rely on, her hero."

There was a long pause that made me turn toward her. She was watching me the way she does when she wants to be certain I've heard her. The she said, "While she's talking about it, she's fussing with her hair and smiling at you a lot. Then once she's sure you're in an agreeable mood, she takes off on a tangent with a little story in which she's made some silly mistake. Like finding her checkbook in the freezer, buying something by mistake at the grocery store, wearing two different color shoes. That's the 'Oh, dopey me,' thing.

"Then when you're sharing a laugh at her expense, she begins looking for something in her purse, or gets up and goes to another room, like she's searching. All this time, she's getting to what she actually wants you to do, and she's talking without looking at you. By the time she's gotten the big request out, but so softly you couldn't hear it, you're puzzled enough to ask what she wants you to do. Then with an expression saying it causes her pain to put the request into words, she tells you she needs a loan, secretly so your dad doesn't know she's spent too much on new clothes; or to get a dent repaired in her car before anyone notices; or any of a hundred other things."

I didn't say a thing when she finished, kept my mouth shut and remembered the time L.G. had to be put away. Guess who was "the only one who could do it," who had to tell his own father it was "dry out and straighten up or she's leaving." Yours truly.

I'd heard every word my wife said back then and never doubted her. Yet even knowing that, all these years later I had let my mother succeed again.

I said, "Convince him to do what, Momma?"

"Honey, maybe it's time for you to get a hearing aid. I just told you, make him see it's time for us to move to a retirement village. Right now. Let him choose which one, so he thinks it's his idea. Cooking and keeping house are wearing me down, especially with him in the family room sitting in his recliner watching John Wayne movies all day every day."

"I don't know anything about retirement places. Besides..." I saw the look on her face. Might as well quit talking. I could easily take him to coffee with me in the mornings and either to dinner at noon or get him to ride with me in the afternoon. Maybe after a week on a cruise to Costa Rica with her sister, Momma wouldn't be so dead set on moving.

I was probably wrong about her changing her mind. By the time she finally left, I'd heard from her six more times. Five times she called, three of those she left messages because I quit answering. The content ranged from "I'm so excited about this trip;" "I'm looking forward to finally getting a rest;" "I just read in the AARP magazine about how older women get stress-related illnesses after their husbands retire;" to "I saw this on Fox News. Living in retirement communities prevents dementia by helping people stay active and engaged. I'm talking about him, not me."

The sixth time was a greeting card she managed to leave in my pickup—one of those "to a special person" ones. She'd written a simple message. Thank you for helping save our marriage. Love, Momma P.S. He thinks he's John Wayne. This morning he told me to get up and cook breakfast. Said I was laying in bed burning daylight.

I didn't even have time to get in the door that morning before Dad said, "Let's go over to Texico and get some breakfast. That café still in business over there?"

On the way to the pickup, I said, "You look mighty shiny this morning. Going someplace in particular?"

"A person ought to have a good breakfast. Keeps the liver functioning, specially if you plan to consume alcohol later in the day. Learned that when I went away for the cure that time."

"All I thought you learned was twelve steps."

He looked toward the sky, not in my direction. "Nice day. Nothing better than a spring day when the wind ain't blowing."

All the way over to that little burg sitting on the New Mexico side of the state line, he commented on the passing scene—condition of cattle grazing on wheat pasture, a new feedlot, the chicken factory outside Farwell. That left me driving and trying to figure out how to bring up retirement villages.

After breakfast, made far too long by his flirting with the waitress, a woman at least my age, he said, "What are we going to do next?"

Passing back across the Texas line made it nine-thirty. With my dad quietly digesting biscuits and gravy, I had time to come up with a new plan. By the time I could drive to the nearest wet county, it'd be ten o'clock so the liquor store there would be open. On Mondays I always restocked. On the way, I'd swing by the north acres and check on my hired hand. I'd told him to shred the turnrows and then make rounds to all the fields and check for aphids on the wheat. Later on I'd set him to work on cleaning out the equipment barn—one more of the things a person does while waiting for the wheat to grow and hoping for rain. I had to check on my helper twice a day minimum or he'd slack off. I figured by the time we eyeballed everything on the north, we'd have covered a hundred miles or so. I'd ease into the retirement village topic after that.

Dad said, "You and that hired man have the place looking good."

"Do you miss it, farming?"

"Not a bit. All that watching, waiting, and cussing the weather plus keeping up with government regulations got to be a pain in the butt. No sir. I was lucky to make enough to retire. It's all yours now."

I saw an opening just before I pulled in at Crossed Keys Liquor. I said, "You deserve to rest and do whatever you want. Both of you. Momma, too."

When I walked out carrying a twelve pack, trailed by the clerk with two thirty-can suitcases, I saw Dad raise an eyebrow. As I started the pickup he said, "They having a sale?" I reached behind into the back seat and wrangled out a Bud. He shook his head when I offered him one. He said, "A little early for me." After a long silence, he said, "That's another reason I'm glad I'm not farming any more. The worse the weather or the markets, the more I drank."

At noon, we went to our house and ate dinner that my wife had ready when we came in. She'd already eaten and left right after we sat at the table, going to the church to practice for next Sunday. She plays organ or piano, depending on the choir director.

You might think he'd have been ready for a nap or a John Wayne movie after we ate. But no, as soon as I'd stowed the beer in the garage refrigerator, he installed himself in the pickup's passenger seat again. Carrying my small cooler, the six can size, I trudged out and loaded up. If we left for Amarillo now, we'd be back in time for supper.

I said, "How do you feel about going to Amarillo?"

"Been there. Don't mind going again if we're back before dark."

So we set out across country toward Amarillo. I always take the back road turning north at Dawn toward Wildorado, driving about fifty-five for forty miles, about one beer's worth. I figured today we'd just drive by, not go in at the retirement village. And I'd start the discussion that way.

We were about twenty miles from home when I realized I'd left the brochures behind. I said, "When I retire, maybe we'll move to Amarillo or maybe Lubbock."

"Jo Bess agree to that?"

"We haven't talked about it. It just something I've been thinking about."

"You might be planning too far in advance. Maybe you won't even have a wife by the time you retire."

That threw me. I said, "You know something I don't?"

He shrugged. "Probably a lot of things"

"I just remembered I need to get out to the Southview place and check on some things. Amarillo'll have to wait." Then I made a u-turn just before the Hereford city limit sign and drove back toward home. When I let Dad out at his house, I said, "Momma told me to remind you to take your pills."

"They ain't nothing but some vitamins. She wants to convince me I'm not healthy, dosing me up. Just as well we come back. I've got some things to do here, too. Same time tomorrow morning?"

I spent the rest of the afternoon occupying myself riding around on the Southview place and finishing off the cans in the cooler.

When I got in for supper, Jo Bess asked if we'd had a good day and what had we done. I said, "We ate breakfast over in Texico and mostly rode around this afternoon, checking on the fields. Wheat's looking okay. Could use some rain."

Later, after we finished eating, she picked up the brochures I'd left on the counter. "You forgot to take these."

I'd told her what Momma had me doing. I said, "It going to be hard to sell him on moving to a retirement place. He's happy the way he is."

"She's not. And I don't blame her. She's eighty years old and shouldn't have to cook and do housework any more. Women don't get to retire. They just have to live with what's left of their husbands."

Before I could say anything, she was out in the garage, making a lot of noise bagging up the empties I'd brought in and set on top of the beer refrigerator. She'd taken to doing that every evening. Then I heard her go in the bedroom and didn't see her again until I woke up in my recliner when the news went off. She was in bed asleep.

Tuesday morning, I was determined to get on the right track. Dad was ready when I pulled up, didn't even wait for me to knock. He didn't act like a guy whose main activity was watching old movies. I hadn't seen him spryer in years. He said, "What's on the agenda today?"

I told him we'd have some breakfast at the Mexican café there in town and then start our rounds out south. And before the day was over, we'd make it to Amarillo. I lied about wanting a new pair of boots from a store there. After we ate and headed south, I popped open my first Bud of the day. He said, "You always start this early?"

"It settles the grease after breakfast. Don't worry. I pace myself. I never aim to get drunk."

"Neither did I."

"You once told me you only went to that hospital and those AA meetings to satisfy Momma. Said alcohol wasn't really a problem."

"Life was the problem. I was the problem."

"Whatever it was, you came back from there acting a lot different."

"Electric shock treatments'll do that. The doctor up there said I was depressed and alcoholic. You might recall I wasn't the only farmer around here agreed to being cured in that place back then. Lots of us running together cultivated some mighty bad habits at the same time we grew some fine crops with all that irrigation water. Working non-stop in the daylight and partying as hard as we could as many nights as we could.

"They'd swear it isn't true, but I think the wives around here tolerated it until one of them got wind there was other women partying with us. That was all she wrote. Like it was one voice, they all said it was get cured or lose everything in a divorce. At least one guy called those treatments a religious experience. Same as being born again."

I said, "To tell the truth, I never did know the particulars."

"I don't remember ever wanting to know much about my parents either."

We were both quiet for several miles. I glanced over at Dad. He was smiling at something private, not looking my way. He said, real softly, "I'll give those gals credit. They had the sense to wait till after wheat harvest that year before they dropped the boom on us."

Later, when we were in Amarillo after I'd bought a pair of boots I didn't need, I said, "I'm going to drive by this place I heard about, a retirement village. Shouldn't take long."

He nodded but didn't say anything. And he didn't balk when I took the tour the woman at the front desk offered. In fact, he said, "Take your time." And when she parked the golf cart we rode around the grounds in back in her space at the office, he even asked her a question—wanted to know how many men lived there. She admitted there were fewer men than women, about thirty in the whole place. He said, "And every one of them popular, I'll bet." She kept the same bright smile she'd worn the whole time.

It was close to supper time when we got home. When Dad opened the pickup door, I said, "Want to go with me to Lubbock tomorrow?"

"Sure. Hadn't had any better offers." He shut the door and then leaned back in the window. "You shaky or anything?"

I held out my hands. "Steady as can be. Why?"

"Just wondered if you get the jitters when you skip your ration of alcohol during the day. You only had the one."

"It's not a requirement, just a minor vice."

"So far." Heading toward his front door, he gave a wave over his shoulder. "See you in the morning."

For some reason, I slept solid and got to Dad's later on Wednesday. "I'd about given up on you," he said. "Everything okay?"

"All good."

We made the rounds of the fields and stopped to give the hired hand some directions he probably didn't need. By one, we were on the outskirts of Lubbock, looking for a barbecue restaurant. We'd talked about barbecue for close to thirty miles and worked up an appetite in the process.

After we ate, me drinking iced tea just to prove I could, I drove on to the place called Lonesome Dove Retirement Ranch without bothering to explain. Another smiling woman, a different golf cart. On a tour which the marketing woman managed to stretch to fifty minutes, I could only find one actual difference between the two places. Lonesome Dove boasted a fully stocked bar and happy hour every afternoon. That brought the only comment Dad made, and then only after we were safely in the pickup. He said, "One thing I can report is that there must be more Baptists in Amarillo than Lubbock."

I couldn't think of any good reason to stay in Lubbock, so I turned back west, wishing all the while for a beer. But I'd left the cooler, empty, in the garage. I reminded myself that reaching for a beer was a habit I could break. Then I thought for a lot of miles about telling Momma I'd failed. It was going to be hard.

Dad spoke up close to the edge of town. "I've had all the fun I can stand today. If you don't mind, I'd like to go to the house."

At his suggestion, we agreed I'd pick him up around eleven the next morning. Fine with me—maybe I'd be visited by an inspiration during the night telling me how to convince him moving to a retirement village was a good idea. Trouble is, I'm no good at selling something I wouldn't buy myself.

Jo Bess listened while I told her what I'd accomplished—nothing other than convincing myself my mission for Momma was doomed. She said, "So you're on his side?"

I guess that made me frown because she came right back with, "Getting mad at me won't fix a thing."

"It's not you I'm put out with. I don't like being put in the middle. They could work this out if they'd just talk to each other."

My wife gave me a long look and then left the room. After I watched the news, I went to bed and ended up staring at the ceiling, trying to remember more of the details of when Dad went for that cure. Mostly what I recalled was feeling like a calf in a squeeze chute, pressed on from both sides, unable to move forward or back.

Thursday morning, Dad opened his front door wearing that blue jogging suit. I said, "You feeling okay?"

"Yeah, sure. Come on in. We need to talk."

He pointed to two Honey Buns on the kitchen table and poured me a cup of coffee and topped off his. I barely had one of the sweet rolls out of its cellophane before he started talking.

"I stayed up late thinking. Your momma's dropped hints about moving for a while now. So it's no mystery to me she put you up to showing me those retirement places. I'm not being stubborn. You know I want her happy. But I know for a fact, I'd shrivel up and die in either one of those places, even if one of them does have a bar. Moving would be a nightmare. She'd have a damn garage sale. Then we'd be cooped up in some place miles from any open country. Full of women and retired preachers. There's got to be some way to make her happy with staying here."

Until he stopped, he'd been leaning toward me, his elbows on the table. Then he sat straight, like he needed the back of the chair to hold him upright. He said, "Some way to make her happy with me."

I filled my mouth with Honey Bun. I wouldn't even let myself imagine them living apart. The roll expanded as I tried to swallow. I poured myself more coffee.

Watching while Dad ate half of his roll, I listened to the repeat of the morning commodity market report coming from the radio in the other room. Wheat still down. Cattle up three cents.

He said, "I'll figure it out. But there's something else you need to know." He leaned forward again and got every bit of my attention by speaking softly. "Jo Bess is going to leave you if you don't straighten up."

Apparently I opened my mouth, because he said, "No, don't start arguing, just listen."

Then he said she had told him she needed his help. He'd be the only one able to influence me. According to her, I was depressed and on my way to being a full-time alcoholic. I only came home to eat and fall asleep in my chair. I never talked to her anymore, and we didn't do anything together. "She started in to tell me details of the things you didn't do together, and I told her I got the picture. So that's why I was on you about drinking beer all day long. Now I've told you, so it's up to you."

He got up from the table like he had a plan, then sat down again. The blue sweat suit hung in wrinkles off his shoulders, bunched around his wrists, as if a muscular man had moved out of it and left him behind. "She went to the trouble to call me to come over so she could tell me all this. She seems serious about it. I didn't ask, but she may have been to a lawyer, son."

I wanted to convince him he'd misunderstood. But first I'd have to fool myself. I just sat there.

After a bit, he said, in the way people talk just to stir the air, "You know, I hadn't noticed until that day, Jo Bess reminds me of your mother. It's the way she makes jokes about herself and how she twists that curl in front of her right ear while she's talking."

He got dressed and we made our rounds and talked about the weather and anything else but what was on our minds after what had been said at breakfast. That afternoon after I let him out at his place, for a couple of hours until near dark, I just drove. According to a sign I passed, I ended up somewhere out near Grady, New Mexico. I stopped and sat still until I had a notion of the way back home. Hell of a note, getting lost forty miles from home.

Friday afternoon late, after a day dedicated to riding around without talking, Dad and I ended up at the old home place, the first farm his parents bought back in 1906. Nothing left out there but the skeleton of an old barn. And the land, of course, the place he'd made me promise never to sell. Before he quit farming ten years ago, we'd planted that whole section back to grass. Deer, dove, pheasants, coyotes, antelope, and assorted other wildlife had slowly repopulated the six hundred forty acres. I drove slowly to the playa near the far north end. It still held some water from the rains last month—a little lake for a little while. When we got close, I stopped, eased the gearshift into park.

With the pickup idling, the sun easing down toward the horizon, the wind slowed to a whisper, we both sat mute for quite a while. That land would never be the way it was before it was first plowed, but it was worth the effort to try.

Then Dad said, "See what you think about this for a plan. What we do is each one of us reports back—you to your Momma, me to Jo Bess. Make it clear we did our very best and it wasn't easy, but that it looks like some things might change. Meanwhile I'll hire someone to cook and clean at our house five days a week and promise to take your momma out to eat on the weekends. Might be able to get that taken care of before she gets back on Sunday evening. And you… well what you do is up to you."

When I let him out at his house, he said, "I expect to be busy, looking for a cook most of the day, but how about Dairy Queen for breakfast first, my treat?"

"It's a deal."

After supper, I helped Jo Bess clear the table. Then I asked if she'd like to take a ride out to the home place. She didn't even ask why, just got a sweater and said, "Okay, I'm ready."

I hoped that by the time we got out there, I'd have an idea of what to say. Parking the pickup where we could see the whole place, with the little lake as a centerpiece, I said, "Remember how we used to come out here, just the two us?"

"Sure I do."

"I miss it." There was a big moon out that cast a glow all the way across the little playa.

She kept quiet. Then after a long time she said, "See how the moon makes a path across the water toward us? It's like a promise of some kind."

I leaned back in the seat. "This is the best the native grass has looked in years."

She put her feet up on the dash. "I've always loved this place. I'm glad you put it back the way it's supposed to be."

It was late when we headed back to town. We took our time.

Made in the USA
San Bernardino, CA
31 August 2017